JOIN THE FUN
IN CABIN SIX . . .

KATIE   is the perfect team player. She loves competitive games, planned activities, and coming up with her own great ideas.

MEGAN   would rather lose herself in fantasyland than get into organized fun.

SARAH   would be much happier if she could spend her time reading instead of exerting herself.

ERIN   is much more interested in boys, clothes, and makeup than in playing kids' games at camp.

TRINA   hates conflicts. She just wants everyone to be happy . . .

AND THEY ARE! Despite all their differences, the Cabin Six bunch are having the time of their lives at CAMP SUNNYSIDE!

MARILYN KAYE is the author of many popular books for young readers, including the "Out of This World" series and the "Sisters" books. She is an associate professor at St. John's University and lives in Brooklyn, New York.

Camp Sunnyside is the camp Marilyn Kaye wishes that she had gone to every summer when she was a kid.

A Witch in Cabin Six

Marilyn Kaye

AN AVON CAMELOT BOOK

CAMP SUNNYSIDE FRIENDS #7: A WITCH IN CABIN SIX
is an original publication of Avon Books. This work has never
before appeared in book form.

AVON BOOKS
A division of
The Hearst Corporation
105 Madison Avenue
New York, New York 10016

First Avon Camelot Printing: May 1990

CAMELOT TRADEMARK REG. U.S. PAT. OFF. AND IN OTHER COUNTRIES,
MARCA REGISTRADA, HECHO EN U.S.A.

Printed in the U.S.A.

OPM 10 9 8 7 6 5 4 3

For Cathy Lesser
and her brilliant ideas

Chapter 1

Megan stood in the center of cabin six, clutching her tennis racket and looking around at the other girls.

"Doesn't anyone want to play tennis with me?" she asked.

"Can't," Katie replied. "Trina and I are playing Ping-Pong with some other girls in the activities hall."

"Sorry," Trina added as she followed Katie to the door.

"Ping-Pong!" Megan called after them. "That's like baby tennis. You should try the real thing for a change." But they were already out the door. She turned to Erin.

"What about you? You want to play?"

Erin shook her head, her long blonde hair bobbing around her shoulders. "I just took a shower, and I'm not getting all sweaty again. Besides, I'm meeting some kids to do make-overs."

"What are make-overs?" Megan asked.

"We're going to try each other's makeup and fool around with our hair."

"What do you want to do *that* for?"

"We're practicing for the Camp Eagle social next week," Erin explained. Then she frowned. "I wish Bobby would ask me to be his date."

Megan's forehead wrinkled. "Are we supposed to have dates for that social thing?"

"We don't *have* to," Erin said. "But it would be nice to have one guy you could count on to dance with."

Megan made a face. "I hate dancing."

"Oh, Megan, you're such a child," Erin murmured as she brushed past her on her way out.

Megan gazed mournfully at her tennis racket. There was still one other person left in the cabin. But there wasn't much chance of getting her to play. Still, it wouldn't hurt to ask.

"Sarah?"

Sarah lay on her top bunk, a book propped in front of her. She probably hadn't even heard the conversation around her.

"Hmm?"

"Do you want to play tennis?"

Sarah was actually kind enough to take her eyes off the page. "Tennis? I can't play tennis, and you know it."

"But I could teach you! We could have regular lessons, and then you could play with me all the time!"

"But I don't want to learn how to play tennis," Sarah said.

"Oh, c'mon," Megan wheedled. "It's fun! You'd probably enjoy it if you tried it."

"I doubt it," Sarah replied. "You have to run around too much."

Megan shook her head in exasperation, but she should have known Sarah would respond this way. She was famous for not taking part in anything too active. "I never get to play," Megan complained, "except when Stewart comes over from Eagle. And that's only once a week."

Sarah had gone back to her book, but at least she was listening. "There must be someone you can play with here at Sunnyside."

Trying to sound as pathetic as she could, Megan replied, "Nobody wants to play with me."

Sarah turned a page. "That's because you always win and they know they don't have a chance."

What she said was true, and Megan knew it. She was the best tennis player at camp. And she

3

had to admit, it was kind of nice being known as the best. But it wasn't worth much when no one would play with you.

Sarah wouldn't be much of a competitor. But giving her lessons would at least get Megan on the court. And it might actually be fun. She tried again. "Sarah, just give it a shot. You're my best friend, right?"

Sarah's eyes didn't leave her page. "Right."

"And best friends do favors for each other, right?"

"Right," Sarah said again.

"Well, you'd be doing me a big favor if you'd let me teach you tennis."

Sarah turned a puzzled face to her. "That doesn't make sense. You'd be giving the lessons, but I'd be doing you the favor?"

Megan nodded. She must have looked really sad and lonely, because Sarah actually put a marker in her book and closed it. "Oh, all right. If it means that much to you."

Megan clapped her hands in glee. "All right!" As Sarah climbed down the ladder, Megan dived under her bed to retrieve her other racket. It wasn't as good as the one she had out, and it was in desperate need of restringing, but Sarah wouldn't notice. Then she located a can of tennis balls. "Okay, let's go."

4

They left the cabin together. Megan wished Sarah would look a little more enthusiastic about the prospect of tennis lessons, but she couldn't ask for the world.

"Erin's making such a fuss about this social at Eagle," Megan noted as they headed toward the courts.

"Maybe because it's the first time they've ever invited us to one," Sarah said. "What do people do at socials anyway?"

"I don't know," Megan replied. "I've never been to one. Erin says there will be dancing. Yuck."

Sarah didn't look very thrilled with that idea either, but for a different reason. "What if no one dances with us? I'll feel so creepy just standing around."

That wouldn't bother Megan at all, but she was sympathetic. "If you really want to dance, I'll get Stewart to dance with you."

Sarah grinned. "I think it's more likely that he'll want to dance with you."

"Yeah?" Megan wondered about that. Stewart was a great tennis partner. And she had to admit, she'd had some fantasies about a romance—but not *now*. Maybe when they were older, like next year. Megan just didn't feel ready for a boyfriend yet.

5

Luckily, there was an empty tennis court available for them. Megan led Sarah to one side and demonstrated how she was holding the racket. "You have to grip it like this. No, lower. No, not that low."

"It's heavy," Sarah complained.

"You'll get used to it. Now, I'll show you how to serve." Megan tossed a ball up and slammed it to the other side. "See? Now you try it."

Sarah threw the ball in the air and swung her racket. Unfortunately, the ball went in one direction and her racket in another.

"Not bad," Megan lied. "Try again."

Sarah did. Once more, the ball and the racket didn't even come close to making contact.

"You have to keep your eyes on the ball," Megan instructed her, "so you'll know where it is."

"But then how will I know where my racket is?"

"You *feel* it," Megan said. "Now, keep trying."

Sarah tried. And tried. And tried again. But the balls just kept coming straight back down.

Megan sighed. "Okay, let's forget about serving right now. I'll serve from the other side, and you just hit it back to me, okay?"

Megan ran over to the other side of the net

and served an easy ball straight to Sarah. It whizzed right beside her—and on past her.

"Sarah! Hit it!"

"I'm trying!" Sarah yelled back.

Megan kept on serving, practically aiming her balls directly at Sarah's racket. But Sarah just flailed her racket blindly in the air. When she actually managed to hit the ball with the edge of her racket, it just bounced down a few feet in front of her. Megan was beginning to lose patience.

"Are your glasses working?" she called out. "Maybe you should get your eyes checked." She came back around to Sarah's side to collect the tennis balls that were strewn all over the court.

"There's nothing wrong with my glasses," Sarah told her.

"Are they slipping down your nose?" Megan asked. "We could get you one of those elastic things to tie them on."

Sarah gave her a sad smile. "I don't think that will help. It's hopeless, Megan. Tennis just isn't my game."

"Nonsense!" Megan replied with determination. "It just takes practice. Don't give up yet."

Sarah briefly closed her weary eyes. "Okay."

Megan went back to her side and began serving balls again. But after three more attempts,

7

she was ready to give up too. Sarah was right. It was hopeless.

"I guess that's enough for today," she said, coming back around. "Let's go get some ice cream."

That suggestion was greeted with more enthusiasm than Megan had seen on the court. Carrying their rackets, the girls headed toward the ice cream stand. They were waiting in line when Katie and Trina came running up to them.

"Guess what?" Katie said. "There's a movie tonight in the activities hall. You're supposed to be twelve years old to get in, but I got special permission for us to see it."

Sarah looked interested. "Is it a sexy movie?"

"No, scary," Katie told her. "It's called *Demon Teen.*"

"Ooh," Sarah exclaimed, "I remember when that was playing at the theater back home. I wanted to go, but my father wouldn't let me."

"It's supposed to be really creepy," Katie said happily. "I convinced Ms. Winkle that we're mature enough to handle it."

"Great," Megan said. She hoped she sounded convincingly eager to see it. But inside, she wasn't exactly thrilled. She didn't much like scary movies. They made her feel—scared.

She remembered the time, just last year,

when she saw this really old movie on television about a man who turned into a fly. He looked just like a tiny fly, but his head was a man's— only no one could see that because he was so small. For ages after that, every time she saw a fly, she imagined it had a human head on it.

She knew she was being silly and letting her imagination run wild, but she couldn't help it. That's just the way she was. Like the time when her baby brother was born, just over a year ago.

She'd just been to a sleep-over party where they'd seen a movie about a baby who was really an evil spirit or a devil or something like that. Somehow she got it in her head that the baby her parents brought home from the hospital wasn't really theirs.

Every time she saw another baby, she'd stare at it, thinking that this one or that one was her real, true brother. And she was always getting the feeling the baby in their house had a weird expression, like maybe he wasn't a real baby. It was a long time before her parents could convince her that they'd brought home a real baby, and he was really theirs.

And then there was that movie in the theater, with the creatures from another planet taking over the world. For weeks after she had had nightmares about that one.

9

"Megan!"

Megan blinked. She wasn't even sure who had spoken.

Trina grinned. "Quit daydreaming and order your ice cream."

"Oh, right." She gave the counselor at the stand her usual order—two scoops of strawberry—and tried not to think about the movie. But it was no use.

She really didn't want the others to know how she felt about scary movies. Maybe she could pretend she was sick or something, she thought, as she licked her ice cream cone. No, they'd know she was faking.

She'd just have to go and get through it. But as they were all walking back to the cabin, she pulled Sarah aside and whispered in her ear. "Tonight, at the movie . . . sit by me, okay?"

For a second, Sarah looked puzzled. Then her wise eyes lit up, and she nodded reassuringly. "Sure. Okay."

Megan breathed a small sigh of relief. Sarah always seemed to understand.

It *was* a scary movie. There weren't any monsters or aliens or human flies or anything like that. What made it so creepy was the fact that the evil demon looked so totally normal.

10

She seemed like just an ordinary sixteen-year-old girl. If you saw her on the street, you'd think she was just an average teenager. She was really cute, and she acted like all the other kids in her high school.

But she had these terrible powers to make people do things they didn't want to do. Pretty soon, everyone in the audience could tell that she wasn't a real girl at all, but a witch in a girl's body.

At first, the things she did weren't that awful. She got a teacher to give her a good grade on a test that she'd actually failed. Then she got the cutest boy at school to ask her to the prom instead of his real girlfriend.

But then she started doing really bad things. Megan watched in horrified fascination as she made another girl she didn't like have a skiing accident. Then, when a teacher scolded her, she made a lighting fixture fall down on her head.

There wasn't too much blood or gory stuff, but the movie still gave Megan the creeps. What really freaked her out was that no one in the movie figured out that this girl was the cause of all the weird situations and accidents going on. Megan felt sure *she'd* know if someone hanging around her was a witch.

When the lights came up, everyone in the

room started talking about the movie. Megan turned to Sarah, who was staring at her hand.

"What's wrong?" Megan asked.

Sarah held out her hand, and Megan gasped when she saw the little semicircular marks. "How did that happen?"

"You did it! Every time you grabbed my hand, you dug your nails in!"

Megan hadn't even realized she'd been grabbing Sarah's hand. "I'm sorry."

"No big deal," Sarah said, rubbing the marks. They joined the other cabin six girls and started back toward the cabin.

"That was a good movie," Trina said. "It seemed so real! You could almost believe something like that could happen."

"How do you know it can't?" Katie asked, smiling slyly. She wiggled her eyebrows up and down. "Maybe you all just *think* I'm Katie Dillon. Maybe I'm really—"

"Katie, stop that!"

Everyone looked at Megan in surprise. "C'mon, Megan," Katie said, "you don't believe in stuff like that, do you?"

"Of course she doesn't," Sarah said.

But Megan was thinking. "There was this new boy at my school last year. And everyone thought there was something creepy about him.

Once, he and I were the last two in a spelling bee. I got this word I knew—but I didn't spell it right." She frowned. "I'm wondering now if maybe he was really a demon and he made me do that."

"That's silly," Erin said in disdain. "You just panicked, that's all. I've screwed up on lots of spelling bees when I knew the words."

She was probably right, Megan thought. But even so, Megan couldn't get the idea out of her head.

Their counselor, Carolyn, was waiting up for them at the cabin. "How was the movie?" she asked them.

"Great," they chorused.

Carolyn must have seen something in Megan's expression, because she then spoke directly, and quietly, to her. "Was it scary?"

Megan shrugged nonchalantly. "Not particularly." And along with the others, she started getting ready for bed.

But as she crawled into her lower bunk, she thought the room looked even darker than usual. And she fervently hoped she wouldn't have nightmares.

Chapter 2

"There's a trip to Pine Ridge this afternoon," Carolyn said at breakfast the next morning. "Are you guys going?"

There was a general bobbing of heads.

"I absolutely *have* to go," Erin announced. When no one asked why, she went ahead and explained. "My parents sent me money for a new dress to wear to the social."

Sarah winked at Megan, and Megan knew what that meant. Erin was making such a big deal over this silly social. But Megan was thinking too that she absolutely had to go to Pine Ridge. It would take her mind off what had happened the night before.

She was still thinking about that dumb movie. And the others knew it—because, in the middle of the night, she'd woken up screaming about witches and demons. Everyone woke up, Carolyn came out of her room, and by the time Megan realized it was just a nightmare, she was so embarrassed she wanted to cry.

No one had said anything about it that morning, which made her feel even worse. And then Katie leaned across the table and spoke in a teasing voice. "Hey, Megan, there goes a real witch for you."

Megan turned quickly. Maura Kingsley, from cabin nine, was walking by. Megan studied her for a minute, then turned back to Katie. "No, she's not a witch. Remember the girl in the movie? She was very nice and normal on the outside. You couldn't tell that she was really evil."

"That's a good point," Katie said, grinning. "Maura's too mean all over to be a witch."

Everyone laughed, including Megan. Katie's good-natured teasing was just what she needed to make everyone stop feeling sorry for her. She attacked her breakfast with gusto, feeling much better.

It was good being here with the girls she'd always gone to camp with. She felt safe and secure with people she knew so well. And as she gazed around the busy, noisy dining hall, she began to relax. Nothing really scary could ever happen at Sunnyside.

And as they went through the normal morning routine, she found herself thinking less and less about the movie. After breakfast, they went back to the cabin and straightened up for inspection. Then they changed into bathing suits and went to the pool.

Darrell, the incredibly handsome swimming coach, gave them their orders for the day. "You're going to work with a partner and practice some lifesaving techniques." Automatically, Katie and Trina got together, and so did Sarah and Megan. Erin paired herself with a girl from cabin seven.

Sarah's swimming had improved a lot that summer, but Megan was still much better. As they practiced the lifesaving moves in the water, Megan knew they weren't really well suited as partners. But that didn't matter. They always paired up together.

After swimming, they went back to the cabin to change. Then there was archery, followed by arts and crafts, then lunch. And finally it was time to go to Pine Ridge.

The cabin six girls all sat together at the back of the camp bus. "I heard there's a roller skating rink that just opened," Katie announced. "You guys want to go?"

"I love roller skating," Megan said.

Trina agreed. "That sounds like fun. I'll go."

"Not me," Erin said. "I'm going to spend the whole afternoon trying on dresses at every store in town." Megan couldn't imagine doing anything more boring, but Erin looked ecstatic at the prospect.

"How about you, Sarah?" Katie asked.

"No, thanks. I was planning to look around the bookstore." She turned slightly to face Megan, with eyes that asked a question.

Megan debated, but only for a few seconds. She owed it to Sarah to hang out with her, after forcing her to play tennis yesterday. "I guess I'll go to the bookstore with Sarah. Besides, if I went roller skating, I'd end up falling all over the place. That's what always happens to me back home." She grinned. "My mother's always saying I was born with scraped knees."

The bus pulled into Pine Ridge and stopped on the main street. "Let's all meet at the ice cream parlor at three o'clock," Katie suggested. Everyone agreed. Katie and Trina took off in search of the new roller rink, while Erin went in the direction of the boutiques. Sarah and Megan headed toward the bookstore.

Sarah's reading habits were always changing. For a while, she was into mysteries. Then she got hooked on romances. Currently, she was reading nothing but science fiction, fantasy and horror, and Megan followed her to that section of the store.

"Wow, look at all these," Sarah said. "And I've only got enough money for two. Help me choose, okay?" She took a book off the rack and read from the back. " 'The special spray was supposed to kill roaches. It didn't. It fed them, and nourished them, and they began to grow—' "

Megan interrupted her with a gagging sound. "Yuck, gross!"

"Yeah," Sarah agreed, and replaced it. "How does this one sound? 'The visitors from the other planet seemed friendly enough. Until they revealed their real motives in coming to Earth.' "

"Sounds boring," Megan said.

"Yeah, I'm sick of alien stuff too. Ooh, wait, listen to this." She grabbed another book. " 'Everyone liked the new family down the block. They seemed to fit in just fine. Until strange and horrifying accidents began to happen.' "

Megan swallowed. "Uh, yeah. I'm gonna go look at comic books." She left Sarah to browse happily on her own.

She couldn't understand why Sarah enjoyed

18

those books so much. Some were silly and unbelievable, like the ones about aliens. And the ones that weren't silly gave Megan the creeps. She wished Sarah would get back into romances.

Of course, romances had gotten them into trouble once, she remembered as she examined the selection of comic books. When their counselor had broken up with her boyfriend, the camp handyman, the girls had used Sarah's romance books as a guide to getting them back together—only to discover that romance books weren't any more realistic than science fiction.

Luckily, this wasn't one of those stores where the salespeople yelled at you for reading and not buying. For the next half hour, Megan pored over copies of *Ultraman*, her favorite comic book hero. He had these neat superpowers, and he only used them to do good things, like rescue people and put out fires.

It would be nice to have someone like that in real life, Megan mused. She envisioned herself on a hiking trip, almost falling off a cliff, hanging onto the ledge. Then—whoosh—Ultraman appears and carries her to safety! Or maybe she'd fall out of a canoe, and Ultraman could save her from drowning. Of course, she probably wouldn't have drowned—she was too good a swimmer.

"Megan, wake up!"

Megan was jerked back to reality by Sarah's voice. "Did you choose your books?"

Sarah held up a bag. "I already paid for them too. What do you want to do now?"

Megan brightened. "Let's go to the sports store. We can get one of those elastic things so your glasses won't fall off when you play tennis again."

"Play tennis again?" Sarah groaned. Megan gave her a meaningful look. After all, *she'd* come to the bookstore for Sarah. Now it was Sarah's turn to go somewhere Megan wanted to go.

Megan loved the sports store. She ran up and down the aisles, looking at tennis rackets, bouncing basketballs, checking out the latest ski equipment. She didn't have the money to buy anything but it was fun just to look.

They found an elastic band for Sarah's glasses. "Can we go now?" Sarah asked as she paid for it.

Megan gazed around the store. She could spend another hour browsing in here. "Where else can we go?"

"Let's go to the ice cream parlor."

Megan checked her watch. It wasn't even two-thirty. "The others won't be there yet."

"So what?" Sarah's eyes gleamed. "We could have one sundae now and another when they get there."

Megan gave her a reproving look. "Two sundaes?"

"Okay, we'll just get a scoop at the take-out window now, for an appetizer."

Megan gave in. Actually, ice cream wasn't such a bad idea anyway. They ambled across the street.

"Those girls in front of the ice cream parlor are staring at us," Sarah whispered.

Megan looked. Sure enough, the four girls hanging out by the store *were* staring at them while whispering among themselves. They all looked about their age. One of the girls in particular grabbed her attention.

The girl had long, straight black hair. She wore jeans and a tee shirt, with an unusual fancy-looking locket hanging down from her neck. But it wasn't her clothes or hair that held Megan's eyes. It was the little black cat sitting on the girl's shoulder.

"What are you staring at?" the girl asked suddenly as Sarah and Megan approached the take-out window.

21

Megan jumped. She hadn't realized her interest was so obvious. "Oh, sorry. I was just looking at your cat."

The girl grinned. "What's the matter? Haven't you ever seen a cat before?"

"Sure I have," Megan replied. "I've just never seen anyone carry a cat on her shoulder."

Another girl smirked. "I guess you rich Sunnyside girls have servants to carry your pets around for you." The other girls started giggling.

"How did you know we were from Sunnyside?" Megan asked.

"Oh, just a wild, crazy guess," the black-haired girl said, and their giggles turned into hysterical laughter.

"Our tee shirts, dummy," Sarah hissed.

Megan reddened. She'd forgotten they were wearing Camp Sunnyside tee shirts.

"For your information," Sarah told them, "we're not even allowed to have pets at Sunnyside. And we don't have servants either."

"Oh you poor thing," one of the girls said, her voice dripping with sarcasm. "You have to spend the whole summer at your country club without servants."

"Sunnyside isn't a country club," Megan retorted.

"Oh no?" another girl said. "Don't you have

a big swimming pool and tennis courts and your very own private lakefront that no one else is allowed to use?" She turned to her friends. "Sounds like a country club to me." And they all nodded in agreement.

Megan and Sarah exchanged looks. This wasn't the first time Pine Ridge girls had made fun of Sunnyside campers, calling them rich kids and snobs. They'd heard stories of girls who had had unpleasant encounters with Pine Ridge girls.

"Uh, excuse me," Megan said. But as they passed by, Megan clearly heard one of them say, "Summer girls. Yuck. Why don't they stay out at their dumb camp where they belong?"

Megan and Sarah tried to ignore the girls as they stepped up to the take-out window.

"What can I get you?" the waitress at the take-out window asked.

"One scoop of chocolate chip with sprinkles, please," Sarah ordered.

"I'll have a scoop of strawberry, please," Megan said.

"Sorry, we're out of strawberry."

Megan settled for vanilla. The town girls, still giggling, finally went away, and Megan turned to Sarah. "Why do those town girls hate us?"

Sarah dug into her ice cream. "I don't know.

I guess they think we're a bunch of rich snobs or something."

"Us?" Megan was amazed at the mere thought. "That's crazy. We're not rich and we're not snobs. Okay, maybe Erin is, a little. But the rest of us aren't any different from those Pine Ridge girls."

"True," Sarah said, licking her spoon. "But they don't know that."

"Because they don't know *us*." Megan flattened her ice cream with her spoon, making it mushy. "It's too bad. I don't like thinking that people hate us when we haven't done anything to make them hate us."

Sarah scraped the sides of her paper cup to get every last drop. "Well, there's nothing we can do about it."

Megan ate a spoonful of ice cream, trying to pretend it was strawberry. Then she swallowed. "Maybe there *is* something we can do about it!"

"Like what?"

As the idea developed in her head, Megan got excited. "We could ask Ms. Winkle if we can have a special day for town girls to visit the camp. Then they'd see we're not a bunch of rich snobs."

Sarah considered this. "Hey, that's not a bad

24

idea. In fact, it's better than not bad. It's really good."

Katie and Trina came up, and they all went into the ice cream parlor. It was a cute, old-fashioned looking place, with bright red booths and a long counter with stools that swiveled. The girls settled into a booth and Megan told them her idea.

"That's a super idea," Trina enthused. "I hate the way those girls look at us every time we come to town. This way we could become friends."

Katie agreed. "You know, Megan, when you manage to get your head out of the clouds, you can be pretty smart."

"Oh, c'mon," Megan protested. "I don't daydream all that much."

The hoots that greeted this remark told her otherwise. Just then, Erin ran in, clutching a bag. "You guys aren't going to believe what just happened," she said breathlessly.

"You just found the most fantastic dress in the entire universe," Katie replied in a bored voice.

"Well, yes, I did, but's not what I'm talking about. I just saw Bobby! He was here in town with some Eagle campers. And guess what?"

She paused dramatically. "He asked me to be his date for the social!"

Megan knew Erin expected to hear gasps and screams and cries of joy, but all she got was some polite smiles. "That's nice," Trina said.

"Yeah," Sarah echoed. "Very nice."

"Is that all you can say? *Nice?*" Erin sighed in resignation. "I should have guessed you guys could never appreciate something this important."

Katie rolled her eyes. "Erin, if you want to hear something really important, listen to the fantastic idea that Megan's come up with."

Once again, Megan explained her plan. But Erin's thoughts were elsewhere. "Yeah, that's okay. Look, I'm going to run over to the shoe store and see if I can find some to match this dress. And I need new nail polish too. I'll be back in a few minutes."

As she ran out, Sarah patted Megan's arm. "Never mind her. Believe me, your idea's better than okay."

Megan didn't mind. She was used to Erin. And she was too excited about her idea to care. "Yeah, I know. I just hope Ms. Winkle thinks so too."

"You girls must have ESP," Ms. Winkle said to the group gathered in her office. "We've been planning to start a day camp program for Pine Ridge girls. And a Visiting Day would be the perfect way to get people interested. What gave you this idea, Megan?"

Megan told her about the girls making mean remarks by the ice cream parlor. "It happens all the time," Katie added. "I think the town girls have bad feelings about us."

The camp director nodded. "Yes, I'm aware of that. And I think a Visiting Day would be helpful in improving relations, as well as giving prospective day campers an opportunity to see Sunnyside."

"Then we're really going to do it?" Megan asked.

"Absolutely," Ms. Winkle replied. "I'm going to make arrangements immediately with the Pine Ridge Community Center to notify their membership. We'll have our Visiting Day on Saturday. You girls can help me plan it. And Megan, I want to thank you for your excellent idea."

Megan basked in the smiles of approval that were aimed at her. Maybe this would make them all forget how babyish she'd acted the night before. And now, with Visiting Day to plan and new day campers to meet, she wouldn't have time to think about that silly scary stuff anymore.

Chapter 3

Bright and early Saturday morning, Megan and Sarah headed to Ms. Winkle's office for last minute instructions. Passing the field where they'd be having the big cookout, they saw the huge banner they'd help paint the night before. In big red letters it proclaimed WELCOME, NEIGHBORS!

"How many girls are coming?" Sarah asked.

"Twenty," Megan reported. "And some of their parents are coming too, to look the camp over. Ms. Winkle's hoping they'll sign their kids up for day camp."

There were representatives from each cabin in Ms. Winkle's office. The camp director, looking just a little more flustered than usual, gave them a pep talk.

"We want our guests to see Sunnyside at its

best. So I know you'll all be especially friendly to these girls. Make them feel welcome and show them a good time. Whether or not they decide to become day campers here, we want them all to leave with good feelings about Camp Sunnyside. Now, to make sure that each visiting girl gets a good personal introduction to our camp, I'm assigning each cabin a girl or two who will be your special responsibility."

She then called out each cabin number and gave them a card with the name of the visitor they'd be hosting.

"How will we know which girl is which?" someone asked.

"They'll be wearing name tags," Ms. Winkle said.

"I've got an idea," Megan piped up. "Each cabin could make a sign to hold up for each girl. Like, our's would say, WELCOME"—she consulted her card—"TANYA."

Ms. Winkle gave her a smile of approval. "Excellent idea. That will make each girl feel special. Now, they'll be arriving at noon. First we'll have the cookout, and then you'll show your girls around the camp."

"What did you say our girl's name is?" Sarah asked as they left the meeting.

Megan looked at the card again and read

29

aloud. "Tanya Gibbons, age eleven. I hope she's nice."

Sarah nodded. "But even if she isn't, we'll just bombard her with the Sunnyside spirit, and she'll have to like this place."

Megan gazed at her in admiration. Sarah could make friends with just about anyone. She remembered when Ms. Winkle's niece, Jackie, had stayed in their cabin for two weeks. She'd acted like a tough hoodlum, really mean and nasty. But Sarah had believed there was a good person behind that angry exterior, and she'd finally broken through Jackie's act.

Of course, Megan planned to knock herself out being friendly to this Tanya. And she figured Katie and Trina would be nice to her too. She couldn't be sure about Erin. If the girl didn't live up to Erin's definition of cool, Erin might be just a little snotty.

But more than anyone, Megan knew she could absolutely count on Sarah. She was just unusually sensitive to people and their feelings.

Megan was excited at the prospect of Visiting Day—and a little nervous, considering it had been her idea. She was so anxious for the visitors to arrive that the morning seemed to go on forever. In arts and crafts, she carefully drew a sign saying WELCOME TANYA, and fixed it to a stick so they could hold it in the air. Trina made their sign even more special than the ones other cabins were making, by drawing a border of flowers all around the words.

The cabin six girls were all out on the field before any of the other campers. Even Erin seemed to be in a particularly good mood—though Megan suspected that had more to do with having a date for the social than the new visitors.

Soon all the Sunnyside girls were gathering on the field, carrying baskets of food, helping lay festive yellow tablecloths on the picnic tables, and generally getting everything ready for the cookout. Counselors lit the barbecue grills, and everyone seemed to be in a party mood.

When the bus filled with visitors pulled up, Ms. Winkle blew her whistle. And as the passengers started getting off, the girls held up their signs and joined in singing the official Sunnyside song.

"I'm a Sunnyside girl, with a Sunnyside smile,
And I spend my summers in Sunnyside style,
I have sunny, sunny times with my Sunnyside friends,
And I know I'll be sad when the summer ends,

31

But I'll always remember, with joy and pride,
My sunny, sunny days at Sunnyside!"

As usual, the song gave Megan a special tingle. Surely anyone hearing it would want to be part of this place. She stood on her tiptoes, holding the sign as high as she could, and searched the oncoming visitors for anyone who might be Tanya Gibbons.

With all the noise and activity around her, she didn't hear the voice at first. But when she felt Sarah tug at her arm, she turned.

"Hi. You looking for me?"

Megan's mouth opened, but she was totally speechless. She couldn't believe who was standing there. There was no cat on her shoulder this time, but Megan recognized her anyway. It was the girl from the ice cream parlor, the one with the long black hair.

"Megan, say something," Sarah hissed.

"Are—are you Tanya Gibbons?"

"That's me!" And then her hand flew to her mouth. "Ohmigosh, you're the girls who were at the ice cream parlor!"

"That's right," Megan said stiffly.

Tanya gave her an abashed smile. "I guess me and my friends weren't very nice to you guys. Sorry about that."

32

Katie, Trina, and Erin were listening to this conversation with confusion all over their faces. "What are you guys talking about?" Katie asked.

Megan looked at Sarah. To her surprise, she was smiling. "Oh, we met Tanya in front of the ice cream parlor last week, before you guys got there. Her friends were teasing us a little. It was no big deal. C'mon let's go get some food."

They all trooped off toward the barbecue grills. Megan was still recovering from the shock of seeing Tanya. But she knew the whole point of this day was to make friends with these girls, so she made an effort to be friendly. "My name's Megan." Then she introduced the others.

Tanya smiled sweetly at them all and told them how nice it was to meet them. They collected their hamburgers, and then went to the long table where the potato salad, cole slaw, and all the other food was set out.

"This is really nice," Tanya said. "My parents said if I like it here, I can come as a day camper for three weeks."

"Oh, you'll like it," Sarah assured her. "Sunnyside's fantastic."

Trina echoed this. "We've got horses, and canoeing, and a pool."

33

"And tennis courts," Megan chimed in. "You don't play tennis by any chance, do you?"

"Are you kidding? I *love* tennis!"

Megan was extremely happy to hear this. "Great! I've been needing someone to play with."

Sarah pretended to look insulted. "Hey, what's wrong with me?"

Megan grinned. "Sarah, you're my best friend, but I have to say you're not the best person to play tennis with." She turned to Tanya. "I tried to teach her, but—"

"I'm hopeless," Sarah finished cheerfully.

"Oh, come on, no one's hopeless," Tanya said. "You probably just need practice."

"No, thanks," Sarah said. "I'm not the athletic type anyway."

"We'll show you all around the camp after we eat," Katie told Tanya.

Erin was staring at the medallion around Tanya's neck. "That looks like real gold."

"I think it is," Tanya said. "It's very old. It first belonged to my great grandmother." She fingered it. "According to my mother, she was a Gypsy."

"A Gypsy?" Megan looked at her askance. "Don't Gypsies have magical powers?"

"Don't ask me, I never met my great grand-

34

mother. But my mother remembers her, and she told me my great grandmother used to read palms and tell people's fortunes—stuff like that." Tanya grinned. "I think maybe I inherited that from her."

"Can you tell fortunes?" Sarah asked, her eyes wide.

"Sure," she said, her pale green eyes sparkling. "I'll tell yours later, if you want."

She's teasing, Megan decided. Either that or showing off. The others looked impressed, though. As they all ate and talked, Megan took the opportunity to study this unusual girl.

Tanya sort of *looked* like a Gypsy, with her long, straight hair and those hoops in her ears. Now that Megan could take a closer look at that thing around her neck, she could see it was elaborately carved with a strange-looking design. There was something mysterious-looking about it.

Tanya was asking them lots of questions about what they did all day. Sarah finished her hamburger first and went back for dessert.

"It's chocolate cake," she announced happily on her return.

Tanya turned to Megan. "I'll bet you wish it was strawberry ice cream."

"How did you know I like strawberry ice cream?"

"Because I heard you order it at the ice cream parlor."

"Oh, right. And they were out of it."

Tanya nodded. "I knew they'd be."

Megan eyed her sharply. "How'd you know that?"

The girl grinned. "Because they're always out of one flavor or another."

"Oh." Megan chewed the last of her hamburger and gazed at Tanya thoughtfully. "I'm going to get some cake."

When they were all completely stuffed, they started off on a tour of the camp. Tanya seemed practically awed by everything she saw. She exclaimed over the beauty of the lakefront, admired the horses, oohed and ahhed over just about everything.

"She's really sweet," Trina whispered to Megan.

"Yeah, she seems to be."

"What do you guys do when it rains?" Tanya asked.

"Oh, there's lots of indoor things to do in the activities hall," Katie said.

Megan looked up at the blue, cloudless sky. "At least it's not going to rain today."

"You can't be too sure of that," Tanya noted.

What an odd thing to say, Megan thought. They started toward the arts and crafts cabin. They were about halfway there, when the sky went dark, there was a crack of thunder, a flash of lightning—and suddenly it was pouring rain.

The girls dashed the rest of the way. Once inside, everyone just stood there, dripping. "Yuck," Erin complained. "I'm soaked." She fingered her wet hair in dismay.

"We're all soaked," Katie said. "Too bad. It was so nice out just a minute ago."

"Weird," Megan murmured, and then she remembered something. When she had said it wouldn't rain, Tanya had said not to count on that. And then it *did* rain. That was strange. . . .

Sarah was gazing out the window. "It's just a summer shower. It'll be over in a few minutes."

"Well, since we're stuck in here, maybe Tanya can tell our fortunes," Katie suggested.

Sarah brightened. "That'll be fun. Me first!"

"Okay," Tanya said. "Sit over here." She indicated a stool, and then pulled another one over so she could face Sarah. "What would you like to know?"

"Um, let me see . . . tell me what I'm going to be when I grow up."

"Okay." Tanya looked deeply into Sarah's

eyes. "You will be doing something creative. Something artistic."

"Sarah can't draw at all," Megan interrupted.

Tanya's eyes didn't leave Sarah's. "I didn't mean she'd be an artist. An actress, maybe . . . no, not an actress. A writer."

Sarah gasped. "How'd you know I wanted to be a writer?" Tanya just smiled.

Erin was watching in fascination. "Tell my fortune," she demanded. She nudged Sarah off the stool and took her place.

"Do you want to know what you're going to be when you grow up?" Tanya asked.

"Nah, I'd rather know something that's going to happen soon."

"Okay." Once again, Tanya made intense eye contact. "I see a boy in your life . . . you're going to have a date with him."

"Wow." Erin looked positively stunned. "I *do* have a date. For the Camp Eagle social next weekend." She turned to the others. "Did any of you guys tell her?"

"No," they chorused. Erin looked back at Tanya. "Wow," she said again.

"My turn!" Katie announced. "Just tell me something good that's going to happen to me. Predict something."

As she got on the stool, Megan turned away. She was tired of watching this. Besides, that expression on Tanya's face when she looked in people's eyes made her uncomfortable. Maybe it was just because she didn't like staring.

Tanya seemed to be having more trouble with this prediction. Finally she said, "You will receive some money."

"Oh yeah? That's good. When am I getting it?"

Tanya's expression was regretful. "I'm sorry. I can't tell you that. But you can expect the money sometime soon. Who wants to go next? Megan?"

"No, thanks," Megan said. When the others looked at her curiously, she searched for an excuse. Luckily, the weather provided her with one. "It stopped raining. Let's show Tanya our cabin."

They all started out, but Megan lingered in the back of the group. Sarah fell behind and walked alongside her. "Is something wrong? You've got this strange expression on your face."

Megan wasn't aware of it. "Really? No, nothing's wrong. I was just wondering . . . how does she do that fortune-telling stuff? I mean, is it a trick of some kind?"

"I don't know," Sarah said. "Maybe it's just common sense. All you have to do is look at Erin, and you know she's the kind of girl who has dates, right? And she heard me talking at lunch about how I don't like athletic stuff, so she just took a guess that I was into creative things."

"But what about Katie and the money?"

Sarah thought about that. "Oh, she probably just figured we all get money from home once in a while. And even if Katie doesn't, she'll get her allowance when she goes home. You notice Tanya didn't say *when* she'd get the money."

"So you think she was just playing games," Megan said.

"I guess so." But Megan didn't think she sounded completely sure of that.

By the time Visiting Day was over and the visitors were escorted back to the bus Tanya had made up her mind about Sunnyside. "I really like this place. And I'm definitely asking my parents to sign me up as a day camper."

"Super!" Sarah cried out, and the others responded enthusiastically too. They waved Tanya off, and started back to cabin six.

"Well, I'd say Visiting Day was a big success," Sarah said. "All those people on the bus

40

looked happy. And we know we've got at least one day camper."

"And we owe it all to Megan," Trina said, throwing an arm around her shoulder. "It was definitely a great idea."

Megan was about to thank her, when Katie suddenly yelled, "What's that?" She practically dived under the bushes that lined the path. When she came back out, she was waving something in her hand.

"It's a twenty-dollar bill!" she squealed.

"One of the visitors must have dropped it," Trina said. "You'd better take it over to Ms. Winkle and see if anyone has reported losing it."

"Oh, I will," Katie said. "But I'll bet no one does report it. And then I'll get to keep it!"

"This is so incredible," Erin said. "It's just like Tanya's prediction! Didn't she say you'd get money?"

"That's right!" Katie grinned. "Okay, it's probably just a coincidence. But I'll take predictions like that any day!"

Just a coincidence, Megan thought to herself. Katie must be right. Still, it was strange that she should find that money today, right after Tanya said she would. And how did Tanya know it was going to rain?

41

Forget it, she told herself firmly. It's just a coincidence, that's all. And maybe if she kept telling herself that, she'd get rid of that funny little doubt.

Chapter 4

"Is Tanya coming today?" Trina asked as the girls were getting dressed for breakfast a few days later.

"Yeah," Sarah replied. "We're meeting her here at the cabin after breakfast. She's going to be following our schedule."

Megan, who was sitting on her bed and pulling on her tennis shoes, looked up. "Oh yeah? How come?"

"I asked Ms. Winkle if she could," Sarah told her. "Since we already know her. And that way we could introduce her to other kids."

"Oh." Megan concentrated on tying her shoelaces. "That's nice."

Her tone wasn't very enthusiastic, and Katie noticed this. "I thought you'd be more excited

43

about her coming. After all, you'll finally have someone to play tennis with."

Megan got up. "Sure, I'm glad she's coming."

"Well, you're not acting like it," Katie remarked.

Megan scowled. "What am I supposed to do? Jump up and down and yell 'goody-goody'?"

She realized they were all looking at her curiously, and she couldn't blame them. She didn't usually make sarcastic cracks like that. And why wasn't she more enthusiastic about Tanya? She seemed very sweet, and easygoing, the kind of person who was ready to make new friends and have fun. There was no reason not to want her to be with them.

She wondered if maybe she was just a little unhappy about having someone new hanging around with the group she knew so well. No, she decided, that wasn't it. She liked meeting new people. And just because Tanya did silly things like tell fortunes was no reason for her to dislike her. She *had* to give this girl a fair chance to fit in.

"I *am* glad she's coming," Megan repeated, with a little more conviction this time. "Maybe she'll want to play tennis with me this afternoon."

Sarah looked relieved at hearing this.

"Maybe. But you should give her a chance to get used to us and Sunnyside before you destroy her in a tennis game."

Megan grinned. "Yeah, I better not trounce her till tomorrow." Feeling better already, she joined the others and Carolyn to go to the dining hall.

The sight of one of her favorite breakfasts—French toast and sausage—cheered her even more. "What do you guys think of the new day camper?" Carolyn asked them as they dug into their food.

"Oh, Tanya's really sweet," Trina said.

"Lots of fun," Katie added.

"And she knows how to tell fortunes," Erin said.

"But that's just for fun," Megan said quickly. "I mean, it's not like she can actually see into the future or anything like that."

"But she told me I'd get some money," Katie noted. "And I found that twenty-dollar bill the same day! Nobody ever claimed it, so Ms. Winkle told me yesterday I could keep it."

"That's just a coincidence," Megan argued.

"And she knew I had a big date coming up," Erin said. Then she tossed her head so her hair bounced on her shoulders. "Of course, I guess that's not so surprising. She might have heard

45

about this social coming up, and just assumed *I'd* have a date for it."

Megan agreed. "You're probably right."

Trina continued. "And when she told Sarah about being a writer someday, well, there's a trick to doing that—figuring out what someone wants to hear and then telling them that's what's going to happen."

"How do you know?" Sarah asked.

"My mom used to tell fortunes, just for fun, at our PTA carnival every year. She'd start off by saying something like, oh, 'There's a man in your life.' And she'd watch the person's expression carefully. If the person looked puzzled she'd say, 'No, there's not a man, but you wish there was,' or something like that. Remember how Tanya stared at you when she was telling her fortune?"

Sarah nodded.

"Well, that was so she could judge your reaction. When she said you'd do something creative, you must have looked interested. When she said, 'an actress,' you didn't, and when she said, 'writer,' your eyebrows went up. So she knew she was on the right track. If you hadn't looked interested, she would have gone on telling you different things until she hit the right one."

"Oh." Sarah actually looked a little disappointed.

"But you don't really believe people have the power to see into the future, do you?" Megan asked Sarah.

Sarah sighed. "Not really. But you never know." She turned to Carolyn. "What do you think?"

Carolyn considered the question. "I think that if you believe in anything hard enough, it seems real to you. I mean, I know people who swear by astrology. And I have a friend who goes to a psychic."

"But you don't think that magical stuff is *real*," Megan persisted.

Carolyn shrugged lightly. "I suppose not. But like Sarah said, you never know."

Megan concentrated on her French toast. She was trying to hide her surprise. She always thought Carolyn was so down-to-earth. She'd figured Carolyn would just laugh at all this magical stuff.

They were back in their cabin, straightening up, when Tanya walked in. "I'm here," she announced unnecessarily.

She wasn't alone. "Wow, what a neat-looking cat!" Katie exclaimed.

Megan looked up. Sure enough, there it was,

47

sitting on Tanya's shoulder just as she'd seen it in front of the ice cream parlor. The solid black cat.

The others gathered around Tanya and her cat. "Oh, she's adorable," Trina cried.

"She makes me miss my cat back home," Carolyn said.

"Can I hold her?" Sarah asked.

"She doesn't like anyone but me to carry her," Tanya apologized. "She might scratch you."

"What's her name?" Erin asked.

"Angel."

Megan thought that was an odd name for a black cat. "Uh, Tanya, we're not allowed to have pets at Sunnyside. Are we, Carolyn?"

"Well, no, we're not supposed to bring them."

Tanya clapped a hand to her forehead. "Oh, no. I knew that, and I forgot! I'm just so used to taking her around."

"You didn't have her at Visiting Day," Megan pointed out.

"She was at the vet."

"Can't we make an exception, just this once," Katie asked Carolyn. "I mean, the cat's already here."

Angel purred, and Carolyn smiled. "Okay, just this once. But you shouldn't take her to the pool. Will she stay here with me?"

Tanya cocked her head so she was looking in Angel's face. "I want you to stay with Carolyn and be very, very good, okay?"

Megan watched this curiously. She knew lots of people talked to their pets. But Tanya acted like she was actually expecting the cat to understand her!

The girls changed into their bathing suits, and they all started toward the pool. Tanya walked between Sarah and Megan. "I'm not a very good swimmer," she confessed.

"Neither am I," Sarah told her.

"In fact," Tanya continued, "I'm really crummy."

Sarah grinned. "I'm worse."

They were acting like being bad swimmers made them special friends, Megan thought. "Listen, if you need any help, just ask," she told Tanya.

"Or ask Darrell," Sarah said. "He's the swimming coach. And he's gorgeous." She went into the usual swoon the girls all did when they heard Darrell's name. Megan did it too, but without her usual spirit.

At the pool, Darrell wanted them to continue working on their lifesaving skills. "Pair up and get into the pool," he yelled.

Megan had been talking with Katie. Automatically she turned to join Sarah. To her surprise, she saw Sarah and Tanya already in the pool—and obviously, paired up.

Megan stood there, totally confused. Darrell saw her. "Megan, team up with Gayle," he called out. Megan obediently joined the cabin five girl, whom she didn't know very well. They got in the pool, and Megan went through the motions of the lifesaving routine. But her thoughts were elsewhere.

Why did Sarah do that? They always worked together at the pool. Okay, maybe she just wanted to make Tanya feel welcome, but she didn't have to be her partner. Darrell would have found her someone.

Maybe she was making a big deal out of nothing. But she couldn't help it. She felt a little hurt.

As soon as their session was over, she motioned to Sarah, who joined her on the landing. "What's the matter?" Sarah asked, looking totally innocent.

"Why'd you pick Tanya for your partner?"

Sarah shrugged. "Gee, I don't know. It just sort of happened. I was standing there, and she was standing there, so when Darrell said to pair up, it just seemed natural."

"But you and I are always partners in swimming."

Now Sarah looked a little abashed. "Yeah, I know. Funny, I didn't think about that. I'm sorry."

"It's okay," Megan said. Sarah really did seem sorry. "I mean, it's not that important."

Sarah nodded. "Actually, being partners with Tanya is better for me. You and I weren't very equally matched."

Megan's eyebrows shot up. "You want to keep on being her partner?"

"If you don't mind," Sarah said. Abruptly, Megan turned away.

"Wait a minute," Sarah called after her. Megan stopped and let her catch up. "You're not really mad, are you?"

Actually, she was. But it sounded awfully babyish to admit. Finally she relented. "No. I'm not mad." Beyond Sarah, she saw Tanya watching them. She forced a smile. "Listen, you want to meet me during free period? Play checkers or something?"

She knew she was suggesting checkers because only two people could play.

"Well, I told Tanya I'd show her around," Sarah said, "but that won't take long. I'll meet

51

you in the activities hall around three-thirty, okay?"

Throughout the morning, Tanya was enthusiastic about everything, even archery, which no one liked all that much. And she always seemed to be smiling. At lunch, standing in line for their trays, Katie asked, "What are we getting today?"

Trina looked to see what the girls emerging from the kitchen were carrying. "It looks like chili."

Megan was surprised. She couldn't remember ever getting chili at Sunnyside before. And that had never bothered her, because she didn't like chili very much.

But Tanya was pleased. "Yummy! Chili's one of my favorite foods in the world."

Lucky for Megan, there were cheese sandwiches to go with the chili, so she could fill up on those.

There was another surprise waiting for her when they all went to the stables after lunch. "I haven't ridden much before," Tanya told them.

"You should take Starfire," Katie said. "She's very gentle, and she'll do anything you want her to do."

Megan was more than surprised to hear this.

She was stunned. Of course, Katie was usually a generous person. But not when it came to Starfire. It was generally accepted that Starfire was Katie's horse. Megan thought it was very strange that she would offer her favorite horse to this stranger.

They had arts and crafts next, and then it was free period. "I'm going to show Tanya around the campgrounds some more," Sarah told Megan. "But I'll meet you in the activities hall for checkers in half an hour."

"Okay," Megan said, and she went off with Katie and Trina to get ice cream. On the way, she couldn't help asking Katie about what she'd done in the stables. "How come you let her ride Starfire? You never let any of us ride her."

Katie looked thoughtful. "I don't know. I guess I was just trying to be helpful."

"But there are other gentle horses she could have ridden," Megan persisted.

"Why are you making a big deal about this?" Trina asked. "I think it was very nice of Katie to give her Starfire."

There was nothing Megan could say about that. Trina was right. It *was* nice of Katie. But not very natural.

After she had her ice cream, Megan headed over to the activities hall to meet Sarah. She set up a checkerboard on a card table, and sat down to wait. And wait. And wait.

Finally she looked at her watch. It was after three-thirty. Where was Sarah? She was always so punctual. Just then Erin walked in with some of the older girls.

"Erin, have you seen Sarah anywhere?"

"Yeah, she's down at the tennis courts. With Tanya."

Megan's mouth fell open. Sarah—at the tennis courts? That was *really* weird. She jumped up, left the building, and ran all the way to the courts.

Sure enough, there was Sarah on one side of the court. Tanya was on the other side. Megan stood silently behind the gate. Tanya's cat was there, and she rubbed herself along Megan's ankle. But Megan ignored her and watched the court.

Tanya served the ball, and it flew over the net. Sarah ran forward—and hit it back. Then Tanya slammed it over—and Sarah returned it. They weren't strong shots, and the ball didn't exactly fly over the net—but the racket was meeting the ball, and for Sarah, that was a miracle.

Megan watch in disbelief. Then Sarah saw her. "Megan, hi!" She looked at her watch. "Oh

no, I forgot. We were supposed to play checkers!"

Megan went onto the court. "How did you
learn to hit the ball?"

"Tanya's been showing me how. She's a really good teacher."

Tanya walked around the net and joined
them. "Isn't Sarah doing well?" she asked
proudly.

"Yeah," Megan said. "Really well. It's funny,
though. I was trying to teach her last week, and
she couldn't hit the ball at all."

Tanya smiled that charming smile of hers.
"Maybe she just needed a little more practice."

"Oh, no, it's not that," Sarah said. "It was the
way you explained it, showing me how to watch
the ball and all that."

I showed you how to watch the ball, Megan
wanted to say. But it would sound like she was
starting an argument. "It's too late to play
checkers now," she said.

"Well, why don't we go for a walk?" Sarah
said. "We could show Tanya the woods."

"I'd like that," Tanya said. She scooped up
her cat and placed her on her shoulder.

"Okay," Megan said. The three of them left
the court and started up the hill. Just then, Megan stumbled. It happened so fast she couldn't

stop herself. Suddenly she found herself on the ground.

"Are you okay?" Sarah said anxiously, kneeling down next to her.

"Sure," Megan said faintly. She couldn't figure out what she had tripped over. There weren't any rocks or tree stumps around.

But as she started to get up, she clutched her ankle. A stab of pain had just shot through it.

"Oh no!" Tanya cried. "You didn't break it, did you?"

Sarah helped Megan stand, and Megan tested putting the injured foot on the ground. "I don't think so," Megan said. "I wouldn't be able to stand if it was broken."

"You should go to the infirmary anyway and have the doctor look at it," Sarah told her. "Do you need help getting there?"

Megan tried walking a few steps. There were twinges in the ankle, but as long as she didn't put too much pressure on it, it didn't hurt so much. "No, I can make it. I'll see you guys later."

She limped over the infirmary. Someone was in the office with the doctor, so she settled down in the waiting room. To pass the time, she picked up a magazine some camper had left lying there.

Tales of the Supernatural was the title. Not exactly her kind of reading, but she had to do something so she opened it. Most of it looked pretty dumb—stories about vampires and were-wolves and people who had seen UFOs. But something in the table of contents caught her eye—an article called "All about Witches."

She began reading it. And as she read, she found herself totally caught up in it. The article reported that witches were usually charming and friendly, but they could cast spells on people without anyone realizing it. They could cause people to do things and act in ways that weren't normal for them.

She skipped over the part about the special witch groups, called covens, and their rituals and holidays. But then she got to another part that interested her.

According to the article, witches frequently had some sort of special talisman, a charm, which enhanced their powers. And they usually had something else, too. A cat, preferably black, which the witch called her "familiar." A witch could use her cat to aid her in displaying her powers.

Megan's stomach began to jump. A special charm. A black cat. Tanya had both.

A cold, frightening chill ran through her. This

explained everything. Why it had rained on Visiting Day, and why Katie found the money. It explained why Sarah had chosen Tanya for her swimming partner and why Katie had offered her Starfire. Why Sarah could suddenly play tennis.

Tanya had magical powers. She could make things happen. She was getting them to do things they wouldn't normally do. This even explained why they'd had chili for lunch, when they'd never had it before. It was Tanya's favorite, and she'd cast a spell on the cook.

And this explained why Megan had fallen just now. Tanya must have sensed Megan's uncertain feelings about her. She must have realized that all her charm and friendliness didn't fool *her*. So she made Megan fall—just to get rid of her, so she could have Sarah all to herself on the walk. Maybe so she could cast more spells on her.

It was an incredible notion. And Megan's head was swimming at the very idea. But it had to be true. There was no other explanation.

Tanya Gibbons was a witch.

Chapter 5

In the doctor's office, Megan barely felt the doctor wrapping the elastic bandage around her ankle. Her mind was in a state of confusion as she pondered her suspicions about Tanya. Was she letting her imagination run wild again? A witch at Sunnyside . . . it sounded so preposterous.

After all, lots of people had cats. And lots of people wore lockets. But what about all the weird things that had been happening? All the clues were there. And they added up to only one thing.

"There you go," the doctor said. "It's just twisted. Stay off it for a day and it'll be fine."

Megan barely heard him. "Thanks," she murmured, and left the office. Her ankle didn't really hurt, but she felt a little twinge every now and then. And each time she felt the twinge, she saw Tanya's face in her mind.

It was all so unbelievable. She could just imagine what the others would say if she told them. Actually, they probably wouldn't say anything at all. They'd be too busy laughing at her.

No, she would have to wait until she was absolutely sure. She'd just have to keep her eyes on Tanya and watch for more clues.

At dinner that evening, Sarah raved about Tanya. "She's so neat! She's got a great sense of humor. And she's into *everything.*"

"She catches on quick, too," Katie said. "Like, she'd never shot a bow and arrow before. But the counselor only had to show her once, and she did it perfectly."

Sarah nodded. "I've been doing archery for ages, and I still can't shoot an arrow straight. She's amazing."

"Amazing," Megan echoed. "Didn't you think it was kind of strange that she hit the bull's-eye on the target with her very first try?"

"Beginner's luck," Katie said.

"Sounds like Tanya's made a big impression on you girls," Carolyn commented.

Megan kept her eyes on her food. Big impression—that was an understatement.

"And she's cute, too," Erin said. "We're going

to make French braids on each other this week. Hey, I wonder if she'd like to go to the Eagle social with us."

Now that was very strange, Megan thought. If Erin thought Tanya was so cute, why would she want the competition at the social?

"That's a good idea," Carolyn said. "I'll ask Ms. Winkle if that's okay."

"And then she could spend the night with us in the cabin," Trina suggested.

Megan looked up in alarm. Overnight—in cabin six? "But where would she sleep?"

"She could have my bed," Katie said. "I'll use my sleeping bag on the floor."

Megan couldn't believe what she was hearing. Everyone was being so generous. They were all acting like they'd do anything for this girl!

But the more she thought about what they were saying, it all began to make sense. If Tanya was a witch, she probably had the ability to make them all like her. All she had to do was cast a spell or something.

But then something else occurred to her. Why wasn't Tanya's spell working on *her?* If Tanya had the power to make people like her, why did Megan still have bad feelings about her? That *didn't* make sense. She tried to put it all out of her mind and listen to what Katie was saying.

"Now that there's six of us, maybe tomorrow we could have a volleyball game with another cabin during free time."

"I can't," Megan said. "Stewart's coming over from Eagle to play tennis with me."

"Maybe you shouldn't make too many plans for Tanya anyway," Carolyn said. "Why don't you wait and find out what she wants to do."

"Yeah, you're right," Katie replied.

Megan gave her a sidelong glance. Katie was usually so insistent about everyone doing what she wanted to do. The way she'd immediately agreed to hear Tanya's plans—that wasn't like her.

They're bewitched, Megan thought. They're all under her spell. And once again, she wondered why she was the only one who wasn't affected.

The next day, Megan watched Tanya closely. Just like the day before, the rest of the cabin six girls were very chummy with her. But as they went from one activity to another, Megan couldn't honestly say she saw any evidence of magical powers. She was actually beginning to doubt her own suspicions, until something happened at lunch.

"I'm starving," Sarah said as they approached the dining hall. "I hope there's something good today."

"It's Wednesday," Megan reminded her.

"Oh, right. Macaroni and cheese."

"Do you always have the same food on the same day?" Tanya asked.

"Pretty much, when it comes to lunch," Sarah told her. "Like, Monday's tuna salad, Tuesday's hamburgers . . . what's the matter?"

Tanya was wrinkling her nose. "I don't like macaroni and cheese," she said. She was playing with her locket, twisting it around in her hand.

When they entered the dining hall, some girls who had already collected their lunches went by them. Megan glanced at their trays. And then her eyes widened. There was no sign of macaroni and cheese on those plates.

"Oh goody," she heard Katie exclaim. "It's fried chicken!"

While her cabin mates all expressed happy surprise, Megan shivered. "I'll be right back," she muttered, and left the line. She hurried over to the table where Ms. Winkle was sitting.

"Ms. Winkle, how come we're not having macaroni and cheese? We always have that on Wednesdays."

Ms. Winkle looked vague. "Oh, I don't know,

dear. Some of the campers have been complaining about the routine. And the cook just thought it was time to vary the menu." She patted Megan's arm. "Don't worry, dear. We'll be having macaroni and cheese another day soon."

But that wasn't what was bothering Megan. All she knew was that Tanya didn't like macaroni and cheese. And she remembered seeing Tanya holding her locket as she told them this.

No, it wasn't complaints from the campers that made the cook change the menu. It was Tanya.

Megan went back, collected her tray, and joined the others at their usual table. They had already started eating.

"This is delicious," Tanya said, chewing on a chicken leg.

"Yeah, I figured you'd be happy," Megan remarked.

"What do you mean?" Tanya asked.

Megan gave her a knowing look. "Isn't fried chicken your favorite food?"

Tanya seemed puzzled. "I like it. But it's not my most absolute favorite food in the world."

"Wouldn't it be great if all we ever had to eat were our favorite foods," Sarah said. "I'd have pizza every day."

"Yeah," Katie said. "And potato chips. That's *my* favorite. Tanya, what's your favorite food?"

"Chocolate pudding," Tanya said promptly. "I could have that every day and never get sick of it."

"I like anything chocolate," Erin agreed. "I just wish it wasn't so fattening." She nibbled delicately on a piece of chicken. "If I gain any weight at all, I won't be able to fit into my new dress for the social."

"What social?" Tanya asked.

"We're having this get-together with Camp Eagle," Katie explained. "There's going to be dancing." She made a face. "I just hope there's other stuff to do too."

"I'm sure there will be," Trina said. Her eyes twinkled. "But I bet you end up dancing with Justin."

To Megan's surprise, Katie turned a little pink. "Well, maybe once."

"I love to dance," Tanya remarked.

Erin lit up. "Me too! Maybe you can come. Carolyn's going to ask Ms. Winkle. And then you could spend the night in the cabin."

"That would be great!" Tanya replied. "What are you wearing?"

As they all got into a boring discussion of clothes, Megan got up. "I'm getting dessert," she announced to no one in particular. She went back to the kitchen counter. And when she saw what was being laid out there, she felt sick.

Chocolate pudding. Exactly what Tanya would have wished for.

Megan liked chocolate pudding too. But suddenly she wasn't very hungry anymore. She went back to the table. "My ankle's hurting me," she lied. "I'm going back to the cabin to lie down."

Carolyn looked at her in concern. "Do you want me to come with you?"

"No, thanks. I think I just need to lie down for a while."

"What's the dessert?" Sarah asked.

Megan couldn't resist. "Why don't you ask Tanya." Then she turned and headed out.

Back in the cabin, she threw herself on her bed. She wished she could just fall asleep and forget everything, but she had a feeling she'd only dream about fried chicken and chocolate pudding. And Katie saying she might actually dance at the social—that was the strangest thing she'd heard yet! Katie was never interested in that sort of thing.

Just then, Carolyn came in. "Megan, how's your ankle?"

"It's fine now." She forced a grin. "I'm playing tennis with Stewart this afternoon, so I just concentrated on getting rid of it."

"Are you sure it's a good idea to play tennis?"

"It's okay," Megan assured her. "I'll keep the bandage on. And I just won't let it bother me."

Carolyn smiled. "Mind over matter, huh?"

"What does that mean?"

"Some people believe that if you think hard enough about something happening, you can make it happen. Like getting rid of a pain in your ankle. It's the power of positive thinking."

Megan considered this. "What if—what if you really wanted chocolate pudding for dessert, and you made the dessert become chocolate pudding. Would that be the power of positive thinking?"

Carolyn laughed. "No, I'd call that magic."

Exactly, Megan thought.

Stewart was waiting for her at the tennis court. "What happened to your ankle?" he asked, eyeing her bandage.

"I just fell and twisted it. No big deal." Megan gave him a cocky grin. "And it's not going to hurt my game."

"You coming over to Eagle for the social Saturday night?"

"Yeah. I hope there's going to be something for us to do besides dancing."

"You don't like to dance?" Stewart asked.

Megan shook her head vehemently. "Do you?"

Stewart shrugged. "Sometimes . . . c'mon, let's play."

If there was one place in the world where Megan didn't daydream, it was on the tennis court. Her mind hardly ever wandered there—mainly because she knew she had to concentrate to play well.

So it was nice being able to put all her worries and fears about Tanya out of her head, and think only of slamming tennis balls over a net.

Stewart won the first game, but she won the next one. They were just about to start the third, when something out of the corner of her eye distracted her.

Sarah and Tanya were sitting on the slope just outside the court. "Can we watch?" Sarah yelled.

"Sure," Stewart called back. "Hey, Megan, c'mon. It's your serve."

The thought that Tanya's eyes were on her made Megan feel positively queasy. She tossed the ball in the air, swung her racket—and missed. She couldn't remember the last time she'd messed up a serve like that. She tried again. This time she hit it, but it was weak, barely skimming the top of the net.

It was all downhill after that. Her balls flew out wildly, going out of bounds, hitting the net, and half the time she couldn't return Stewart's serves.

What's the matter with me? she thought in a panic. She'd never played this badly before. It just wasn't like her at all. And then, turning to meet the ball Stewart had sent over, she noticed Tanya, playing with her locket.

Megan froze as the ball sailed past her. Tanya's doing this to me, she thought wildly. That's why I can't play. She knows I suspect her. And she's using her powers against me!

It was a horrifying thought, but it made perfectly good sense. It explained why she fell yesterday. And it explained why she wasn't reacting like the other girls to Tanya. Tanya might have cast spells on them to make them like her. But she'd put a curse on Megan.

"Megan!" She realized Stewart had come around to her side of the court. "What's the matter with you? You're acting like you're in a trance or something."

Megan swallowed. "Maybe I am."

"Huh?"

She tried to recover her wits. "Never mind. Look, Stewart, I think I better stop playing. My, uh, ankle's bothering me."

She faked a limp and started off the court. Watching her, Sarah jumped up. "What's the matter?"

"My ankle hurts a little."

"Either of you want to play?" Stewart asked.

"I don't think I'm in your class," Sarah said, with a grin. "But Tanya's pretty good."

"Oh yeah?" Stewart twirled his racket. "Wanna prove it?"

"Sure," Tanya said, jumping up. "Megan, can I use your racket?"

Megan hesitated. The thought of her very best racket in the hands of a witch gave her the creeps. But if she said no, everyone would think she was awful.

Reluctantly, and without smiling, she extended the racket to Tanya. "Thanks," Tanya said, and skipped out to the court.

Sarah moved closer to Megan. "Hey, don't look so depressed. I'll bet even professional tennis players have a bad game once in a while. And it's probably just because of your ankle, anyway."

"It's not my ankle," Megan stated. She took a deep breath. "It's Tanya."

"What do you mean?" Then her puzzled expression cleared. "Oh, did it make you nervous having her watch you?"

"Not exactly." She paused. "Sarah, haven't you noticed anything strange about her?"

"Like what?"

"She didn't want macaroni and cheese for lunch. And it wasn't. She wanted chocolate pudding for dessert. And it was."

The puzzlement on Sarah's face returned. "So?"

"Think about it," Megan persisted. "Yesterday I was going to walk with you two. But I fell, so I couldn't. And then today I couldn't play tennis."

Now Sarah looked totally bewildered. "Megan, I don't have the slightest idea what you're getting at."

"Remember the movie we saw? About the girl who could put spells on people and make them do what she wanted them to do?"

Finally, Sarah caught on. "Megan, are you saying you think Tanya is—a witch?"

Silently, Megan nodded and watched anxiously to see if Sarah was going to start laughing.

She didn't. But she rolled her eyes and looked at Megan as if she'd lost her mind. "Honestly,

71

Megan. You've come up with some nutty ideas before, but this takes the cake. First of all, there aren't any witches, not real ones."

"How do you know?" Megan shot back. "Just because you haven't known one personally before doesn't mean they don't exist."

Sarah shook her head. "Even if there were witches, Tanya isn't one. She's a perfectly nice, normal girl. And I don't know why you don't like her. Everyone else does."

"That's because she's put spells on all of you. And I think she's put a curse on me."

"Oh Megan, that's crazy. You're letting your imagination run wild again."

Megan opened her mouth to object, but Sarah wouldn't let her. "Now, I want you to put this idea out of your head right this minute. And I promise I won't tell the others what you said."

"All right, don't believe me," Megan muttered. "But just wait. You'll see."

Sarah was about to say something, but just then Stewart and Tanya joined them. "Hey, you're pretty good," Stewart was saying to her.

"Thanks," Tanya said. "You want to play another game?"

"I can't," Stewart said, and Megan could hear the regret in his voice. She looked at him, hard. Had Tanya cast a spell on him too?

"I have to meet my bus," Stewart explained. "Are you coming to the social at Eagle on Saturday?"

"I hope so," Tanya replied. "I love to dance."

"Well, maybe I'll see you then. Bye, Megan, Sarah." And Stewart took off.

He didn't even ask me how my ankle was feeling, Megan thought glumly. Sarah got up off the ground. "Let's go get some ice cream. C'mon, Megan."

Megan got up. "No thanks. I'm going to the cabin." She held out her hand for the tennis racket, and Tanya gave it to her.

"Thanks for letting me use it," Tanya said.

Megan didn't even bother with, "You're welcome." She turned and started up the slope.

She wouldn't have minded some ice cream right then. But there was no way she was going to spend any more time than absolutely necessary around Tanya.

Besides, she'd be afraid to eat ice cream with her. It could be poisoned.

Chapter 6

Right after dinner on Saturday, Megan sat on her bed and watched her cabin mates in amazement. From the way they were behaving, you'd think they were getting ready for Cinderella's ball.

Sarah was on Trina's bed, applying pale pink polish to Trina's nails. Above them, Katie was vigorously rubbing her black patent leather shoes with a cloth. Erin, wearing her new dress, was still fussing with her hair. Then she went to the nightstand next to her bed, where two perfume bottles stood. She put a drop of one on her left wrist, and a drop of the other on her right. Then she went over to Megan and extended her arms out.

"Which one smells better?"

Obligingly, Megan sniffed. "They smell exactly the same to me."

"Oh, Megan." Then Erin frowned. "Don't you think you'd better start getting ready?"

"I don't think I want to go," Megan said.

This got everyone's attention. "Megan, you have to go!" Katie exclaimed.

"Why? I don't want to dance, and I don't feel like getting dressed up."

Waving her hands in the air to dry, Trina turned to her. "Megan, Carolyn's made plans to go into Pine Ridge with another counselor. If you don't go with us to the social, she'll have to stay here with you. You don't want to ruin her evening out, do you?"

Megan sighed. No, she didn't want to do that to Carolyn. Reluctantly, she got off the bed and went to the closet. "Maybe I'll just wear jeans."

"You can't wear jeans to a social," Erin scoffed. She joined Megan at the closet. "Here, wear this." She pulled out a flowered sundress.

Megan eyed it in distaste. But she took it from Erin and started to change.

"Megan, what's the matter?" Trina asked. "You seem so down."

Megan caught Sarah's eyes. She could tell Sarah was afraid she was now going to announce all her feelings about Tanya. But she wasn't about to do that. If Sarah, her best friend, wouldn't believe her, why would she think any of the others would?

"It's nothing," she said. "I don't feel like going to this thing, that's all."

"You're just worried no one's going to ask you to dance," Erin teased.

"I am not! I don't even want to dance!"

"Well, I do," Sarah said. "And I *am* afraid of being a wallflower."

"Don't worry," Katie advised her. "If no one else asks you, I'll get Justin to." She came down from her bed. "Erin, could you put these barrettes in my hair?"

Megan started feeling even more depressed. It was so hard to believe that these girls she'd known for years could be so interested in a dumb social. Of course, she knew Erin would be like this. But seeing Sarah, Trina, and especially Katie fussing over their looks and talking about who they were going to dance with made her even more convinced that something bizarre was going on. It had to be Tanya who was making them act like this.

Carolyn came out of her room. "You all look so lovely! I have to get my camera and take a picture of you." She ran back in her room and emerged a second later with the camera.

At that very same moment, the cabin door opened and Tanya came in. "Oh, you're just in time!" Carolyn said. "Everyone, let's go outside and I'll take pictures."

"Tanya, you look fabulous," Erin gushed.

"You look great too!" Then they were all complimenting one another. Megan had to admit Tanya did look pretty. She had her glossy black hair pulled back and gathered in a ruffled hair clip. And the simple, short white dress she was wearing made her look sweet and innocent.

Boy, can appearances be deceiving, Megan thought. She followed the others outside, and Carolyn arranged them for the picture. "Megan, smile!" she commanded. Megan managed a feeble imitation of one.

Then it was off to the bus which would take them to Eagle. Outside the bus, some of the older girls from cabin nine were standing around. Maura Kingsley looked the cabin six girls over and gave them her usual smirk. "Oh, don't you all look precious in your little party dresses." Some of her friends started giggling.

Megan ignored them. But she heard Tanya whisper to Sarah, "Who's she?"

"Don't pay any attention to her," Sarah whispered back. "She's the meanest girl at Sunnyside."

77

Megan watched hopefully as Maura started up the steps into the bus. Maybe Tanya would make something terrible happen to her now—like, fall off the steps and get her dress all dirty. But nothing happened.

Too bad, Megan thought. For once, Tanya's powers could have been put to good use.

It was a short trip around the lake to Camp Eagle. The bus stopped in front of their recreation hall, and the girls piled out.

"Wow, get a load of this!" Katie said. The boys had obviously gone to a lot of effort. The room was decorated with blue and red streamers, helium balloons, and colored lights. At one end there was a long table covered with platters of snacks. A counselor in one corner was putting a record on a turntable, and soon the room was filled with the sound of the latest George Michael album.

At first, the girls all stayed together at one end of the room. At the other end, the boys stood, looking uncomfortable. A few of them were jostling one another, as if daring them to be the first to cross the floor.

This is so dumb, Megan thought. She scanned the group on the other side for Stewart, but there were so many boys she couldn't spot him in the crowd. "Are we just going to stand here like this all night?" she grumbled.

"No," Erin said. "Watch this." She fixed her eyes on her friend Bobby, and smiled. It worked. Seconds later, Bobby, with a couple of friends, crossed the floor. Erin and Tanya met them halfway. And then everyone was mixing.

A boy came over to Sarah. "Want to dance?"

"Me?" Sarah squeaked.

"Yeah, you!"

Sarah looked positively ecstatic as she followed him onto the dance floor. Justin came over with a friend, and they paired off with Katie and Trina. Megan stood there with them for a minute, but she couldn't stand the way Katie was giggling and Trina was blushing.

She went off in search of Stewart. She found him, pouring himself some punch. "Hi," he greeted her. "You want some?"

"Sure," Megan said. She accepted the cup. "Hey, have you heard anything about the big tennis tournament in New York?"

"Yeah, I watched some of the quarter finals this afternoon. We have a television room over there." He indicated a door near the table.

"Who won?"

"That German kid. It was a great match." He started describing it to her, talking loudly so she could hear him over the music. "We get this cable sports channel, and they're going to be showing highlights from the game in a little while. We could go in there and watch if you want."

"Yeah, great!" Watching a tennis game on TV sounded like a lot more fun than watching her cabin mates acting goofy over boys. She was just beginning to think that maybe this social wouldn't be so awful when she heard an ominous voice. "Hi, Stewart."

"Hi, Tanya. Glad you could make it."

Tanya smiled brightly at them. "This is great! I'm so glad I could come. None of the other day campers got invited. I'm lucky I'm hanging out with such a great cabin."

Megan felt like throwing up. What a good act this girl could put on! "I'm hungry," she announced, and turned away from them. She busied herself selecting a cupcake from a tray. "Stewart, you want a cake?"

But there was no answer. When she turned, she saw Stewart and Tanya, on the dance floor. Annoyance churned inside her. Was *everyone* going to be taken in by this witch?

She felt stupid just standing there by herself. She made her way around the room, searching for someplace to hide and sit this thing out. She located a door with a handwritten sign on it that read LADIES ROOM. She pushed it open and went inside.

The bathroom was empty, thank goodness. Megan examined her reflection in the mirror. Her freckles seemed to be more noticeable than usual. Was that because of the awful yellowish lighting in the room? Or was it because she was unusually pale?

An awful thought struck her. In the movie she saw, the witch teen made her rival get sick so she couldn't go to a dance. Was Tanya going to make her get sick?

The longer she considered that, the stranger she began to feel. She touched her forehead. Was it her imagination, or did it feel a little warm?

The door swung open and Erin walked in. "What are you doing?" she asked.

"Do you think I look pale?"

Erin studied her. "No. But a little blush on your cheeks wouldn't hurt. I've got some you could borrow."

"No, thanks."

"Are you sure?" Erin grinned. "You may need all the ammunition you can get."

"What do you mean?"

"I just saw Tanya dancing with your boyfriend."

81

Megan rolled her eyes. "First of all, he's not my boyfriend. He's just a friend who happens to be a boy. I'm not interested in him *that* way."

Erin began applying blush to her already pink cheeks. "I hope you mean what you say. Because it looked to me like Tanya was really casting a spell on him."

Megan stared at her. Were the others beginning to catch on? She spoke carefully. "Then . . . you think Tanya's got some sort of . . . special power?"

Erin laughed. "Yeah, in a way. She's almost as good at flirting as I am! C'mon, let's go back out there."

Well, she couldn't stay in this bathroom all night. Megan followed Erin out. Tanya was still dancing with Stewart. And Stewart had the goofiest expression on his face.

He's entranced, Megan thought in despair. She's done it to him too. All around her, she saw kids dancing, standing in little groups talking, or hanging out at the refreshment table. And the sadness that engulfed her was like nothing she'd ever felt before.

Sarah appeared beside her, her face flushed and her eyes sparkling. "I've danced with three different boys! And I think one of them sort of likes me!"

"Wonderful," Megan muttered.

Sarah looked at her keenly. "What's wrong?" She looked in the direction of Megan's eyes. "Oh, I get it. Tanya and Stewart." Now her expression was sympathetic. "You really like him, don't you?"

Megan pressed her lips together. No one understood. Not even Sarah. They thought she was jealous!

"Oh, just leave me alone!" Megan turned away and went in search of that television room Stewart had told her about. She found it, and it was empty. Fiddling with the channel, she located the highlights of the tennis tournament. And that was where she spent the rest of the evening.

"How was it?" Carolyn asked as the girls returned to the cabin. "Did you have fun?"

"It was positively fabulous," Erin said. "This guy, Kevin, kept cutting in on Bobby and me. Bobby was furious!" She positively glowed with happiness at the memory.

"You should have seen Katie and Justin!" Trina told the counselor. Katie grabbed a pillow and tossed it at her, but she was grinning.

"It's so weird," Katie said. "I used to think boys were nothing but creepy slime. But tonight, I was acting as silly as Erin! And I couldn't help it!"

"That's because you're growing up," Erin informed her. "Right, Carolyn?"

Carolyn's mouth twitched, as if she was trying not to laugh. "Well, I guess that's a way of putting it. Tanya, did you dance?"

Tanya nodded. "Mostly with Stewart, Megan's friend." She turned to Megan. "I hope that was okay. He told me you don't like to dance. I don't want you to think I was trying to steal him from you or anything like that."

"I don't own him," Megan replied. "He can dance with anyone he wants to dance with." Or anyone who *makes* him want too, she added silently.

"You all must be exhausted," Carolyn said. "I know I am. So everyone get to bed. I'll see you in the morning."

When she went back into her room and closed the door, they all got into their pajamas. But no one was ready for sleeping. They were all still feeling silly and giddy. Megan crawled into her bed and watched them sadly.

"Megan, you're not going to sleep, are you?" Sarah asked.

"What else am I going to do?"

84

"Let's tell ghost stories," Katie suggested. "If we're quiet, Carolyn won't hear us."

That was the last thing on earth Megan wanted to hear. But everyone else liked the idea, and they gathered on Trina's bed. Megan stayed right where she was. But she couldn't help hearing the story.

"It was a dark and stormy night," Katie began, her voice low and mysterious. "The family had just moved into the old house on the hill. What they didn't know was that somebody else already lived there. Somebody who had been dead for two hundred years."

Megan tried not to listen. She shut her eyes tightly and wished for sleep. But it didn't come. And Katie's story made vivid pictures in her head.

When she got to the part where the ghost was controlling every member of the family and making them all do crazy things, she couldn't stand it any longer. She jumped out of bed. "I don't like this story. Can't we do something else?"

"I want to hear how it ends," Erin argued.

Katie looked at Megan with unconcealed annoyance. "Sometimes you're such a ninny."

But even with Tanya in the room, Sarah's sensitivity came out. She must have remembered Megan's nightmare after the movie last week. "I think it would be more exciting if Katie stopped here and finished the story tomorrow. Hey, I've got an idea. Let's play Ouija board!"

That suggestion overrode their disappointment about the story. Ever since Erin bought the Ouija board in Pine Ridge last month, hardly a week went by when the girls didn't gather around it to ask questions.

Erin set the board up. The girls gathered around it and placed their fingertips on the pointer. Katie began. "Oh, spirits," she intoned, "are you with us?"

They didn't have to wait long. Slowly, the pointer edged toward the word YES. Megan always found this amazing, and sometimes she wondered if one of the girls was actually pushing the pointer. But they always swore they hadn't.

"I want to ask the first question," Erin said. "Spirits, of all the boys I know, who is the one who will be my own true love?"

The pointer was still. Then, very slowly, it started to move toward the beginning of the alphabet. "It's going to be Bobby," Erin whispered, "or Alan, my boyfriend back home." But as the pointer approached those letters, it hesitated, and then moved away, landing on *D*.

"*D?*" Erin's forehead wrinkled. "I don't know any guys with a name that begins with *D.*"

"Wait, it's still moving," Katie whispered. The pointer continued, to an *A*, than an *R*, then *R* again, then to an *E*, and then practically raced across the board to the *L*.

"Darrell!" Erin shrieked.

"Shh," Trina said, "you'll wake up Carolyn."

"Darrell, the swimming coach?" Tanya asked.

"I don't know any other Darrell," Erin said. "Wow, do you think this could be true?"

"The Ouija never lies," Katie replied.

"This is silly," Megan said. "He's much too old for you."

"Maybe and maybe not," Erin retorted. She sighed dreamily. "Darrell. Oh, wow."

"I've got a question," Sarah said. "What does Katie think about Justin?"

"It's just going to say FRIEND," Katie insisted. But the pointer had other ideas. It immediately spelled out *L-O-V-E*.

"That's crazy!" Katie cried. "Okay, 'like,' maybe. But I'm not in love with him!"

Erin mimicked Katie's earlier words. "The Ouija never lies."

Suddenly, Megan had an idea. It scared her a

little to even ask the question, but she had to get some evidence, some proof, something that would help her convince the girls when she finally got up the nerve to tell them about Tanya. "Spirits, is there anything spooky in cabin six right this minute?"

Automatically, the pointer went to YES. Megan held her breath as she asked the next question. "What is it?"

The pointer hesitated, as if it was trying to make up its mind. When it did, it moved quickly. And it spelled out WITCH.

"Ooo," Tanya crooned, waving her hands in the air. The others laughed.

But Megan wasn't laughing. There it was—spelled out for all to see. They thought it was a joke. But Megan knew it wasn't. She stared grimly at Tanya. Tanya stared right back, smiling. Megan had the feeling she was laughing at her, taunting her, letting her know Megan would never be able to stop her.

Trina yawned. It was contagious. Soon everyone was yawning. And within minutes, they were all in bed.

The lights were out, but Megan could see Tanya taking off her locket. She put it on the nightstand by Trina's bed. Then she went up the ladder to Katie's bunk.

Megan lay there, her eyes open. The locket. Was that the source of Tanya's powers? Tanya was always holding it, playing with it, twisting it in her hands. It had to mean something.

She waited until all whispers and giggles had stopped, and then she waited longer. Finally, the stillness of the room and the sound of even breathing convinced her everyone was asleep.

Moving slowly, she got out of bed. She tiptoed across the room, carefully stepping over Katie in her sleeping bag on the floor. When she got to the nightstand, Trina stirred slightly, and she froze. But Trina's eyes remained closed.

The locket sat there, glittering. Megan reached out her hand and wrapped it around it. Then she tiptoed back to her bed, and shoved the horrid thing under her mattress.

"It's got to be here somewhere," Sarah said the next morning, looking under Trina's bed.

Tanya was searching behind the nightstand. "It's not back here."

Megan was pleased to see how upset Tanya looked. It was obvious that the locket was very important to her. She pretended to be looking around on the floor. "Maybe it fell off at the dance."

"No," Tanya said, "I remember taking it off last night before I went to bed."

"Hey, maybe the cabin six witch stole it," Katie said.

"Don't joke," Tanya said. Her face was troubled. "That locket means a lot to me."

"It'll turn up," Trina said comfortingly. "When we come back to straighten up after breakfast, we'll find it."

"I hope so," Tanya murmured.

Megan turned her head so no one would see her smile. The locket would never turn up. And Tanya wouldn't be casting any spells today.

Chapter 7

Two days later, Megan woke up with a real smile on her face for the first time in a week. She'd had a peaceful, dreamless sleep, and she felt refreshed and energetic. Sitting up in her bed, she looked around. The others were still sleeping.

Cautiously, she slipped a hand under her mattress. Feeling the cold metal of the locket reassured her. It was still there. And there it would stay.

She sank back on her pillow with satisfaction. For two days now, there had been no weird incidents, no sign of magic. Her cabin mates were still friendly toward Tanya, but they weren't gushing anymore about how wonderful she was. No accidents had befallen Megan. Nothing bad had happened at all.

She had been right. The locket was the key to Tanya's magic. Without the locket, she was powerless.

Megan had to admit that her conscience occasionally bothered her. After all, she had stolen the locket, and stealing was a crime. But she'd done it for a good cause. It was worth the little twinges of guilt to know she had saved her cabin mates from the spells of a witch. And besides, on Tanya's last day at camp, she planned to "find" the locket and return it.

Dressing for breakfast, she whistled a tune. "Hey, you're cheerful today," Katie noted.

"Why shouldn't I be?" Megan asked.

"Well, you've been acting kind of peculiar lately."

That's the pot calling the kettle black, Megan thought. But she nodded. "I was just in a mood. Everything's back to normal now."

To her surprise, Trina came over and hugged her. "I'm glad to hear it. You had me worried."

Megan grinned. "There's nothing to worry about anymore."

On the way to the dining hall, Sarah pulled her aside. "Megan, I'm so glad you're your old self again. I guess you got those crazy ideas about Tanya out of your head."

Megan just smiled. Someday she'd tell Sarah

how she rescued cabin six. But not now. Right that moment, she was enjoying feeling free and not hampered by worries and fears. The sun was bright, the sky was blue, Sunnyside had never looked better, and her friends were the best friends a girl could have.

Even the mushy scrambled eggs at breakfast tasted unusually good. She was wolfing them down when she heard Erin say, "Here comes Tanya."

For once, those words didn't give her a chill. She didn't even bother to look up. And then she heard Katie exclaim, "She brought her cat again!"

Megan's head shot up. There it was, in its usual place on Tanya's shoulder. The black cat. What was it the magazine called it? Her familiar. An animal that could be used to carry out her powers.

Suddenly, it was as if a dark cloud had fallen over Megan. And she was scared.

Carolyn's forehead puckered. "Tanya, I told you not to bring the cat again."

"I'm sorry," Tanya said. "She crawled into my duffel bag and I didn't see her. When I opened it in the cabin, there she was. I had no idea she was in there!"

Sure you didn't, Megan said silently. "You better take her home right now."

Tanya looked stricken. "I can't! My mother dropped me off here on her way to work. If I call her at work and tell her she has to pick me up, she'll kill me!"

"Well, I guess there's nothing you can do," Carolyn said. "But don't let this happen again, Tanya. And keep her out of Ms. Winkle's sight, okay?"

"Okay," Tanya said.

Megan jumped up. "It's *not* okay!"

"Why not?" Erin asked.

"I—I'm allergic to cats."

Sarah looked at her in surprise. "Since when? You never told me that."

Megan backed away from the table. "Well, I am. I can't be anywhere near them. Or else I— I get sick. Really sick."

"But you didn't get sick the last time Angel was here," Katie pointed out.

"I didn't want to make a fuss. But I didn't feel good all that day."

"Oh, dear," Carolyn said. "What are we going to do?"

"Can't Megan just stay away from the cat?" Erin asked. "Maybe she could hang out with another cabin today."

Now Megan could see Tanya's powers at work again. Her own cabin mates would get rid of her before they'd offend Tanya.

She was horrified to see Carolyn nodding. "That's a possibility. You could follow cabin seven's schedule today. I'll go talk to their counselor."

Now even Carolyn was under Tanya's spell. Megan had never felt so alone in her life.

But if the cat was staying, she had to get away. She felt like she was deserting her cabin mates, leaving them to the mercy of Tanya's wickedness. At least she knew the worst Tanya would do to them was make them like her even more. But Megan had to keep her distance. She was the one Tanya had put a curse on. And now that she had her cat to help her, there was no telling what Tanya could do to her.

It was a strange and uncomfortable day. The cabin seven girls were nice, and they did the same activities, just in a different order. But it wasn't like being with her own cabin, her own friends.

She couldn't even sit with them at lunch. Tanya was there, that wretched cat on her shoulder. From across the room, she could see them all laughing and talking. They probably didn't even miss her.

But there was one small benefit to being banished from her group. When cabin seven had horseback riding, there was no Katie to claim Starfire for herself. For the first time in ages, Megan got to ride the beautiful mare. Starfire was wonderful. She was gentle, and she always followed the rider's lead.

She saddled the horse, and checked to make sure the girth was tight. Then she led her out of the stable.

Standing at the horse's left shoulder, she gathered the reins in her left hand. Then she placed her left foot in the stirrup, and with her left hand on the mane, she hoisted herself up and swung her right leg over the horse.

She tugged the reins gently and said, "Giddyap." The horse began trotting at a moderate pace. Bouncing on the saddle, Megan began to relax. Okay, today was a setback. But Carolyn wouldn't let Tanya bring that creature back to camp again. If they could just get through today without anything awful happening, they'd be safe. Without her locket or her cat, Tanya couldn't do anything to them. And she'd only be at Sunnyside one more week. That week couldn't pass fast enough, as far as Megan was concerned.

With the warm sun on her back and the light

breeze blowing her hair, Megan soon felt pretty good. All she had to do was give the reins a slight tug, and Starfire began to gallop. A gentle pull made her slow down.

She had slowed down to an easy trot when she spotted Sarah and Tanya outside the riding area, watching. It was cabin six's free period. As she rode by them, they waved, but Megan didn't wave back. She pretended to be concentrating on steering the horse.

What are they doing here? she wondered. Sarah didn't much like riding horses. Tanya had probably convinced her to come. After all, she had the power to make Sarah an expert horseback rider, just like she had made her play tennis decently.

Well, Megan wasn't Katie, and she wasn't under Tanya's spell. There was no way she'd relinquish Starfire to her. So she steadfastly ignored them as she circled the ring.

But there was something in her that wanted to impress Tanya, to show her she wasn't afraid. She jerked the reins, and Starfire began to trot faster. She jerked them again, increasing her speed to a gallop.

Leaning forward, she took the position of a real jockey. Glancing quickly to the side, she could see them ahead, watching her. But she kept her head forward, her eyes on the track.

And then, suddenly, without any warning, Starfire reared. As the horse went up on his back legs, Megan clung to the reins. But the force was too much for her. Somehow, she managed to pull her feet out of the stirrups before falling to the ground.

She lay there, stunned. She'd never been thrown like that before. And Starfire never threw anyone. Gingerly, she sat up and checked herself. There might be a bruise here and there, but nothing was broken.

A counselor was immediately by her side. "Are you all right?" Megan pulled herself up to her feet. She felt a little shaky, but she knew that was just from the shock. "Yeah, I think I'm okay."

She saw Starfire, who was now ambling to the edge of the ring. "What happened? That wasn't like Starfire."

"This cat ran out in front of him. That was what made him rear up like that."

Megan went numb. "A cat? What kind of cat?"

"I don't know. A black one. Are you sure you're okay? You look sick."

"I'm fine," Megan mumbled. Without another

look at the counselor, she strode toward the edge of the ring, where Sarah was now standing alone. She looked frightened.

"Oh, Megan! Thank goodness, you're all right! When I saw that horse throw you—"

"Where's Tanya?" Megan interrupted.

"I'm here." She turned and saw Tanya, holding Angel. "Megan, I'm so sorry."

"Yeah, I'm sure you are," Megan replied. "You're sorry my head wasn't bashed in."

Tanya gaped. "What—what do you mean?"

Her innocent expression made the fury in Megan grow even stronger. "You sent that cat out there to scare my horse."

Even in her anger, she had to admit Tanya was a good actress. She looked absolutely stunned. "Megan, she jumped off my shoulder! I couldn't stop her!"

Megan's fury turned into rage. "Look, Tanya, you might be able to fool the others, but you can't fool me. I know what you are! And I know what you're doing!"

"Megan, don't!" Sarah pleaded.

But Megan wasn't about to stop. Tanya could have seriously injured her. She could have killed her! It was time for a showdown.

"You sent that cat out on purpose to scare my horse. You *wanted* me to fall."

Tanya pretended to be dumbstruck. Sarah looked like she was in a state of shock. Megan took advantage of their silence to continue her accusations. "You've put spells on my cabin mates, a spell on Stewart, and a curse on me. But you're not going to get away with it!"

"I—I don't know what you're talking about!"

"Sure you don't," Megan sneered. "All right, I'll spell it out for you. You're a witch. W-I-T-C-H. Just like the Ouija board said. Your locket was some sort of magic talisman, and you used it to cast your wicked spells. And after . . ." she was about to say, "after I took it" but she caught herself. "After you lost it, you brought your cat here so you could use your power on us. But I'm on to you, Tanya!"

"Oh, Megan," Sarah moaned. "It was an accident. Can't you see that?"

Tanya was very pale. She was clutching her cat tightly as she backed away from Megan.

"Just get out of Sunnyside," Megan ordered her. "And don't come back!"

With that, she whirled around and marched away.

Chapter 8

All that evening, Megan expected Sarah to confront her, yell at her, tell her she had just done a terrible thing to Tanya. Instead, all she got were occasional reproachful looks. At least she felt sure that Sarah wouldn't tell the others what happened. Sarah might be upset with Megan, but they were still best friends, and best friends never told on each other.

The next morning, after breakfast, they returned to their cabin and straightened up. Carolyn conducted her inspection, the girls changed into bathing suits, and then they sat around, waiting for Tanya.

Only Tanya didn't show up.

Carolyn looked at the clock. "Did Tanya tell any of you she wasn't coming today?"

Megan stared at the floor, but she could feel

Sarah's eyes on her. The others shook their heads.

"Well, maybe she's just late," Carolyn said. "Why don't you guys go on to the pool, and I'll send her over when she gets here."

"Erin, why are you wearing lipstick?" Katie asked as they walked. "It's just going to come off in the water."

"I want to look nice for Darrell," Erin replied. "Remember what the Ouija board said?"

Trina glanced at her in amusement. "Erin, you don't really believe that stuff, do you?"

Erin countered with her own question. "None of you guys were moving the pointer, were you?"

"No," they chorused.

"Then I believe it," Erin stated.

"So do I," Megan said.

"But it's impossible," Trina argued. "A pointer can't just move on its own."

"It wasn't moving on its own," Megan said. "The spirits were guiding it."

"That's ridiculous," Sarah murmured.

"No it isn't," Megan stated. "Look, there are mystical things that happen in the world, magical things that no one can explain. You hear about them all the time! Like—like haunted houses, and UFOs, and . . . and witches." She avoided Sarah's meaningful glance.

"Well, I don't believe in that stuff," Trina stated. "I think there's an explanation for everything. People just don't take the time to figure out what it is."

"I agree with you," Sarah said, in a voice that was a little louder than normal. "I think some people just like to believe in supernatural things. So they talk themselves into thinking they're true."

She was speaking to everyone, but Megan knew the words were directed at her. But she pressed her lips together and ignored them.

"Look," Erin said, "all I know is that the Ouija board told me that Darrell will be my true love."

Katie snorted. "Oh Erin, for crying out loud. You're only eleven—"

"Almost twelve," Erin corrected her.

Katie disregarded that. "And Darrell's old! He's got to be at least twenty!"

"But when he's twenty-six, I'll be eighteen," Erin noted. "The Ouija board didn't say our romance was going to happen right away. And I want to make sure he notices me now, so I'll be on his mind."

But Darrell wasn't at the pool. Some other counselor was there. "Darrell has a cold," she announced. "So you kids are just going to have a free swim today."

"Pooh," Erin said. "Well, at least that means I won't have to get my hair wet." She sat at the edge of the pool and dangled her feet in the water. The others jumped in, and lingered by the side.

"I wonder where Tanya is," Katie said.

Megan chose her words carefully. "Maybe she decided she doesn't really like day camp. Maybe she won't be coming anymore."

"Why do you think that?" Trina asked.

"Well, she's really not like us, is she?"

"What do you mean she's not like us?" Erin asked. "What is she?"

Megan couldn't hold the secret inside her forever. "Look, I know this is going to be hard for you guys to believe. But I've been watching Tanya, and I've figured something out about her." She paused and took a deep breath. "She's a witch."

She expected gasps, horrified exclamations, something like that. But all she got were blank stares. Finally, Trina spoke. "A *what?*"

Megan hoped she could sound as convinced as she felt. "A witch. Like in that movie we saw."

Now she was getting some response. Erin's

mouth dropped open. "That's ridiculous!" Trina exclaimed.

And Katie moaned, "Megan, have you completely cracked or what?" Sarah just sighed heavily and shook her head.

Megan had been prepared for this, and she didn't let their reaction bother her. "I've read about witches. They use some sort of charm to help them. Remember how Tanya was always playing with that locket? And the black cat—that's typical too."

"Oh, Megan," Trina began, but Megan didn't let her continue.

"Look at the facts. I spent a long time trying to teach Sarah to play tennis. She couldn't even swing the racket properly. Then Tanya goes to the court with her, and boom! Sarah's actually hitting balls across the net."

Sarah raised her eyebrows. "Did it ever occur to you that maybe Tanya was a better teacher than you are?"

"You don't think I'm a good teacher?"

"Well, Tanya was a lot more patient than you were."

"Okay, but what about the money Katie found?" Megan asked. "And the food? Tanya doesn't like macaroni and cheese. And we didn't get macaroni and cheese on a day when we al-

ways get it. And then she said she likes chocolate pudding. And what did we get for dessert?
Chocolate pudding!"

"That was just a coincidence," Katie said.

Megan brushed that aside. "She wanted to get
rid of me because she knew I suspected her.
Witches can read people's minds like that. So
she made me fall when I was going to take a
walk with her and Sarah."

"Megan, you trip over your own feet all the
time," Trina noted.

"And she sent her cat out in the riding ring
to make my horse throw me."

"That was an accident!" Sarah cried.

Megan was getting frustrated. "Don't you
guys see how she cast a spell over you? Sarah
picked her for a swimming partner, Katie let
her ride Starfire, and all of you were gushing
over her like she was special or something."

"We were just being nice!" Katie said. "She
was new and we were trying to make her feel
comfortable."

"She even put Stewart under her spell! He
was dancing with her all night at the social!"

"But you told Stewart you hated to dance,"
Erin pointed out. "What was he supposed to
do?"

"And she looks like a witch!" Megan continued. "With that long black hair, and that black cat, and that weird locket . . ."

Erin tossed her head. "People are always telling me I look like a movie star. But that doesn't make me one."

Trina faced Megan directly with a very serious expression. "Megan, you've got a wild imagination, and you know it. I guess that silly movie set you off thinking like this. But this is all something you've concocted in your head. Tanya is not a witch."

"How do you know that?" Megan persisted.

"Because there's no such thing as a witch!" Trina stated.

"That's *your* opinion," Megan shot back. She looked around the group. "Don't any of you believe me?"

No one replied, but they didn't have to. She could see the answer in their faces. Even Erin, who believed in the Ouija board, was looking at her as if she were nuts.

Megan turned away and, without another word, she started swimming.

With strong, steady strokes, she swam to one end of the pool, turned, kicked the wall, and swam back to the other end. Back and forth she went. But even underwater, Trina's words rang in her head. "It's all in your head. It's all in your head."

Was it possible? Could she have been wrong? But the facts, the clues . . . they all added up. Okay, maybe her cabin mates found a reason for everything that happened. But how could she be sure?

She didn't know what to think, what to believe. Yesterday, everything seemed so clear. Now, nothing made sense.

Well, maybe it didn't matter. Tanya was gone. And pretty soon everyone would forget about her, and they'd all be back to normal.

Still, the confusion stayed with her, and all morning she felt like she was in a fog. She went through the motions of the day's activities, barely speaking to her cabin mates. At lunch she picked at her food, not even aware of what she was eating. She knew Carolyn was watching her curiously. But it was a cabin six rule never to discuss arguments among one another in front of a counselor.

"Hi, everyone!"

Megan looked up and gasped.

"Tanya, where have you been?" Carolyn asked.

"I had to go to the dentist," Tanya said.

"Well, next time let us know you're going to

be late so we won't worry," Carolyn told her. "Now, go get yourself some lunch."

Megan faked a sudden interest in her food. The other girls fell silent too, with occasional furtive glances in her direction.

Carolyn couldn't help noticing this. "Is something going on I should know about?"

When no one answered, she smiled. "Okay, cabin secrets. But you guys know I'm here if you need to talk."

Tanya returned with her food, and sat at the opposite end of the table from Megan. Except for Erin, whose eyes darted back and forth between Tanya and Megan, everyone acted like nothing had changed.

"What are we doing after lunch today?" Tanya asked.

"Canoeing," Katie told her.

"Great!" Tanya said. "I've never been in a canoe before."

Megan was pleased that they had canoeing too, but for a different reason. She and Sarah could share one. And she wouldn't have to be anywhere near Tanya.

But Sarah had other ideas. After lunch, they went down to the lakefront where the canoes were tied up. Katie and Trina immediately grabbed one and started untying it.

"I'll go with Erin," Sarah announced. "And Megan can be with Tanya."

"What?" Megan and Tanya exclaimed in unison.

"It makes sense," Sarah said calmly. "Tanya's never rowed before, and Megan's very good at it. C'mon, Erin."

Left alone, Megan and Tanya just glared at each other for a minute. Tanya looked annoyed, but Megan was more than just angry. She was terrified. Was she really going out in a canoe with Tanya? *Alone*, with a witch? Her whole body went cold. She couldn't take her eyes off Tanya's eyes. They held her—and they seemed to be challenging her, daring her. Megan swallowed. She wasn't going to let this—whatever-she-was scare her.

She went over to the canoe. Untying it, she realized her hands were trembling, and her doubts resurfaced. Should she just flat out refuse? No, the others would gang up on her. They'd say she was being babyish and mean. They'd tell her she didn't have the Sunnyside spirit. They'd all hate her.

She summoned up every ounce of courage she could find inside of her. You can handle it, she told herself. You can battle a witch.

Besides, what could Tanya do to her? She

didn't have her locket or her cat. She didn't look strong enough to throw Megan overboard—and besides, Megan was an excellent swimmer.

Tanya joined her by the canoe. Silently, they both got in, and Megan used her paddle to push the canoe away from the dock. Without looking at Tanya, Megan spoke. "This is how you use the paddle."

She looked to see if Tanya was doing it right. Naturally, she picked up the movement and rhythm immediately. They drifted out into the lake.

For several minutes, neither of them spoke. Then Tanya asked, "Do you still think I'm a witch?"

Megan shrugged. She wasn't about to speak to her. She had to concentrate on being strong, to fight off any evil force Tanya was directing her way.

"I knew you didn't like me, but I couldn't figure out why. I guess that explains it."

Megan didn't reply. Tanya was obviously trying to distract her, so she could cast a spell.

"And you really think I put a curse on you?"

Megan remained silent. She gritted her teeth and shut out Tanya's voice. But she was aware of her heart pounding. Hard as she tried, she couldn't keep a sense of panic from coming over her. Danger was near. She could feel it.

"Wow, we're practically in the center of the lake," Tanya said. "I can barely see the shore." Then, to Megan's horror, she started to rise.

Megan gasped. What was she doing? Didn't she know what happened if you stood up in a canoe? In a flash, her mind supplied the answer. Of course she knew! She was doing this on purpose!

"Sit down!" Megan shrieked, but it was too late. The canoe tipped over.

Luckily, Megan had time to get a big gulp of air before going underwater. She flapped her arms to push herself back up to the surface. But she didn't move. And in that instant, she realized her foot was caught under the seat of the upside-down canoe.

Still holding her breath, she struggled to free herself. But she couldn't even get a grip on her foot.

Unable to hold her breath much longer, she panicked. Her thoughts raced wildly. I'm drowning! Tanya—the curse—it was true! Tanya was making this happen!

And then she felt a hand on her trapped foot, tugging at it. Suddenly it was free. She felt an arm wrapped across her chest, and then she was being pulled upward. Her eyes were shut, but she felt the air on her face. She gasped for breath as her body was pulled through the water.

The next thing she knew, she was lying on the bank of the lake, coughing. She opened her eyes slightly, but her vision was so blurry she closed them again. But in that brief moment, she had a quick vision of people around her.

She heard Trina's voice. "I'll get Carolyn!"

"Does she need artificial respiration?" That was Katie.

"No. No, I don't." That was her own voice—weak and shaky, but her own.

"Megan, Megan, are you all right?" Megan opened her eyes. Now she could see, and she looked up at Sarah. Her best friend's eyes were filled with tears.

"I'm okay." She struggled to pull herself up. "But now, do you believe me? She almost made me drown!"

"Oh, Megan." Sarah knelt to the ground next to her. "It was Tanya who saved you."

Chapter 9

Wrapped in a blanket, huddled on her bed, Megan gratefully accepted the cup of hot chocolate from Carolyn. Across from her, on Trina's bed, Tanya sat wrapped in a blanket too. She peered at Megan over the top of her cup.

"Are you feeling better?"

"Yes. Are you?"

Tanya nodded. Around them, the others were still talking about the near-drowning and rescue.

Trina still looked shaken. "At first, when I saw the canoe tip, I wasn't worried. I mean, we've all tipped over before. But when Megan didn't come back up—"

"I thought my heart would stop," Erin said, clasping a hand to her chest in a dramatic gesture.

"And we were so far away from you guys," Sarah said. "Not that I could have been much help. I'm not that good at lifesaving yet."

"It's a good thing Tanya knew the technique," Carolyn said. She looked pretty pale herself.

"But I wouldn't have known it if I hadn't had that lesson last week at the pool," Tanya said. "I'm lucky I pick up on stuff like that pretty quickly."

"You really do learn fast, don't you," Megan said in wonderment. It wasn't magic or supernatural power that gave Tanya her ability. It was talent—and brains.

"Can I leave you girls for a minute?" Carolyn asked. "I need to let Ms. Winkle know how you are. She was very upset. There was supposed to have been a lifeguard at the lake, like there usually is. But there was some sort of mix-up, because of Darrell being sick."

"We're fine," Tanya said. "Aren't we, Megan?"

"Yes. We're fine." And Megan knew they both meant "fine" in a way that didn't just mean their health.

She couldn't take her eyes off Tanya. It was as if that dip underwater had cleaned her own brain. That wasn't a witch sitting over there.

115

That was a regular person. A regular person who had saved her life.

And suddenly, she was very ashamed. "Tanya?"

"Yeah?"

"Thank you."

"You're welcome," Tanya said. "I'm sorry I stood up in the canoe. I didn't know you weren't supposed to do that."

"It's my fault," Megan replied. "I should have told you." She paused, and then added, "I'm sorry."

"That's okay," Tanya said.

"Not just about that. About—you know."

Katie was listening to this conversation with undisguised interest. "Did Tanya know you thought she was—"

"A witch," Megan finished. "Yeah. I feel really stupid. I guess sometimes I do let my imagination run off with me."

"That's the understatement of the century," Erin said.

Megan got off her bed and placed her cup on the nightstand. Then she reached under her mattress.

Tanya gasped. "My locket!"

"I thought it was the key to your power." Just

116

saying those words made Megan feel silly. And once again, she said, "I'm sorry."

Tanya was nice about it. "I understand. I'm just glad to have it back." Megan brought it over to her, and fastened it around Tanya's neck. Then she looked at it closely. It was just a locket. Nothing more.

"But there are still some things I don't understand," Megan said. "Like the social at Eagle. I knew Erin would be into that stuff, boys and dancing and all that. But Sarah, you never acted like you were interested in boys before."

"I guess I'm getting interested," Sarah admitted.

"And Katie, you used to hate boys!"

"Yeah," Katie said. "I know. I'm starting to change my mind though. I don't know why."

"It's natural," Erin stated. "You'll get interested too, Megan. If you ever grow up."

Megan took a moment to stick her tongue out at her before asking the last question. "And what about the Ouija board? When it spelled out 'witch'?"

Katie bit her lip. Then she grinned. "Okay, I'll confess. I moved the pointer. You were acting so silly about my ghost story, I decided to give you a little scare." She looked abashed. "I guess that wasn't a brilliant idea."

"No kidding," Trina remarked.

"Wait a minute," Erin said. "Were you moving it when I asked about my true love?"

"No," Katie said. "I figured you were doing it."

Erin shook her head. "Then it must be true!"

"Don't get too excited." Tanya smiled sheepishly. "I did that."

"Then who pushed the pointer when Sarah asked about me and Justin?" Katie demanded to know.

"That was me," Sarah admitted.

Katie grabbed a pillow and aimed it. Then she put it down and started laughing. It was contagious.

They were still giggling when Carolyn returned. "Well, you all look back to normal."

"We are," Megan said. "We're all completely normal." Tanya grinned at her.

"By the way, Megan," Carolyn continued, "When I looked up your file on the computer in Ms. Winkle's office, I saw that it didn't say anything about your allergy to cats."

"Cats?" And then Megan remembered. It was the excuse she'd used to stay away from Tanya.

"So I added it to your file," Carolyn reported. "I'm going to dig up some clothes for you to

118

change into, Tanya." She went into her room. Megan waited until her door had closed.

"I hope my parents never see that file."

"Why?" Tanya asked.

Megan grinned. "Because they'll wonder how I've survived at home. With three cats."

And once again, the cabin filled with hysterical giggles.

MEET THE GIRLS FROM CABIN SIX IN

CAMP SUNNYSIDE #8
TOO MANY COUNSELORS
75913-6 ($2.95 US/$3.50 Can)

In only a week, the Cabin Six girls go through three counselors and turn their cabin into a disaster zone. Somehow camp without their regular counselor, Carolyn, isn't as much fun as they thought it would be.

Don't Miss These Other
Camp Sunnyside Adventures:

(#7) A WITCH IN CABIN SIX   75912-8 ($2.95 US/$3.50 Can)
(#6) KATIE STEALS THE SHOW   75910-1 ($2.95 US/$3.50 Can)
(#5) LOOKING FOR TROUBLE   75909-8 ($2.50 US/$2.95 Can)
(#4) NEW GIRL IN CABIN SIX   75703-6 ($2.50 US/$2.95 Can)
(#3) COLOR WAR!   75702-8 ($2.50 US/$2.95 Can)
(#2) CABIN SIX PLAYS CUPID   75701-X ($2.50 US/$2.95 Can)
(#1) NO BOYS ALLOWED!   75700-1 ($2.50 US/$2.95 Can)
MY CAMP MEMORY BOOK   76081-9 ($5.95 US/$7.95 Can)

AVON Camelot Paperbacks